With trembling fingers she opened his letter

Tears blurred Tamsin's eyes as she read the message within, and she almost wished she had burned it unopened.

"Tamsin, beloved," David had written, "I must see you. Come to me as soon as you can."

Tamsin was torn between love and duty. She was in love with David, but she had been promised since childhood to his cousin Everard. And now her bridegroom was returning from abroad and her wedding date was set.

The marriage must take place.

Fortune's Folly

LISA MONTAGUE

A MASQUERADE FROM

W🌐RLDWIDE

TORONTO • LONDON • NEW YORK • SYDNEY

Masquerade edition published May 1982
ISBN 0-373-30089-1

Originally published in 1981
by Mills & Boon Limited

Printed in Canada

CHAPTER
ONE

AT FIRST sight the conservatory bordering the length of the great ballroom appeared unoccupied. The ideal place to smoke a good cigar in peace and sip some palatable champagne, thought the tall gentleman in dark, exquisitely-cut evening clothes. He set the glass on a ledge and with some relief drew off the white gloves. Why were they always so constricting? Besides, this evening, they seemed almost a waste of time: a cursory inspection of the ballroom had not revealed any young females whom he would be bothered to invite to dance . . . but etiquette demanded the wearing of gloves whether or not the wearer chose to dance.

His second glance, however, made him forget cigar, wine and gloves for it revealed a girl's slender form amid the shadows cast by the forest of potted palms and flowering shrubs, her back towards the double doors through which he had just entered as if she strove to ignore the gaiety and brightness behind them. Certainly, she had no notion she was being minutely observed.

Rather wistfully she gazed through the windows, trying to see what lay beyond this last evening of April 1851. *Yet what can I hope for when my own future was signed, sealed and delivered long ago*, she demanded of herself, without expecting any answer.

Rain was falling. Trembling candle flame caught at the droplets and transformed them into gems so that the panes resembled beaded screens obscuring the real world outside and reflecting only the transparent image of a girl in a rose-coloured ball gown.

Now and then, as phrases of one of Herr Strauss's beguiling melodies floated into that glazed ante-chamber, the toes of her white satin boots tapped long-ingly in time with the music and she raised slim unadorned arms and swayed as if in the embrace of some invisible dancing partner. The grey eyes shone mistily and the lips were half open as if to receive a tender kiss. The silken bell of skirt, with the bunches of gauze roses stitched among its scalloped flounces, dipped and swayed like a flower in a summer breeze. The glossy ringlets hanging from beneath the neat headdress of Honiton lace bobbed against the curve of white neck.

Unwittingly, she made a most bewitching picture.

The gentleman cast a connoisseur's eye over the small straight back tapering to a diminutive waist and the pale shoulders and arms that were almost opalescent in the dim light. An appreciative smile curved lips half hidden between a dark moustache and a fashionably pointed little beard. Nothing, he thought, is quite as charming as beauty observed without the fair possessor being aware, so that she does not immediately modify her figure and expression into what is regarded as correct for an un-chaperoned young female on suddenly being confronted by a gentleman.

What the devil can this nymph be doing here all alone? I'd wager she could have her pick of partners and need not play the wallflower in the conservatory. If I'd seen her in the ballroom I'd have hastened to put my name on her ball card as many times as she and her mamma would permit . . .

Oh how much Tamsin yearned to waltz.

Her reflection gave a discontented little pout.

It seemed so unfair that this small pleasure, as so many others, was denied her by Aunt Scott's rigid code of behaviour.

For there was no hope of treading so much as one movement of the quadrille on this or any other evening until the laggard Sir Everard Fortune returned to England and offered Miss Thomasina Kate Lucas his hand in matrimony as well as to the dance.

Aunt Scott would never have permitted Tamsin—or, Thomasina, as she chose to address her—to stand up with any gentleman however well-born. Was not her niece already spoken for? One glance at this forbidding female dragon corseted into proud purple satin would have dissuaded even the boldest of St Georges from inviting Tamsin to dance.

It was not proper—how Aunt Scott relished that phrase—for any young lady on the brink of a formal engagement to dance with a man save a relative . . . or her future husband. To flout this rule would be to incur the whisper of scandal, something which must be avoided at any price. For a young female with a less than pristine reputation could not be deemed a desirable catch, particularly when she was without money of her own.

As Tamsin had neither living male relatives nor her own money and Sir Everard had proved himself such a reluctant suitor, she had at this Eve of Exhibition Ball, as at all others Aunt Scott had unwillingly allowed her to attend, been forced to sit out every dance while other young ladies gaily waltzed and polkad their way across the floor before the watch of dowagers and chaperones seeking some slight indiscretion—naturally committed by someone else's girl—which might be teased into a tongue-wagging scandal. No young lady, jealous of her good name, mindful of her mamma's strictures and anxious to make a good marriage, could afford to dance more than twice with any gentleman unless there was an understanding.

But, oh how much everyone hoped some miss would bend the rules of propriety.

Thus, while others enjoyed themselves, Tamsin had kept her own eyes modestly cast down lest Aunt Scott somehow divine how occasionally her niece's thoughts entertained the delicious impossibility of just which gentlemen would have selected her as a partner. But, of course, she would never have the chance of finding this out, just as she was never to know what it was to fall in love and be loved in return. But those were matters she scarcely dared dream of let alone allow space for in her waking thoughts. . . .

The gentleman had quite forgotten about the champagne, and his desire to smoke had long since evaporated. He studied the girl closely, and with precise movements replaced the cigar in its golden case. His curiosity was aroused. Suddenly, he shook his head as if remembering.

How fortuitous. He had found her again. Never would he forget that charming toilette. Now the Ball need not be such a dreary occasion.

Swiftly, as if he had instantaneously made up his mind, the man stepped forward. Almost before Tamsin's ears heard his steps, he had caught her by the waist, and whirled her about, enfolding her in strong arms which pinned her close against him. Passionately, he pressed his lips down upon her open mouth, a mouth that had never before received a man's kisses.

She would have screamed but for that mouth which seemed to drink in her breath and demand a total surrender of her person, her senses, even her identity. Terror and the scent of Russia leather and macassar-oil threatened to overwhelm her and cast her into a dangerous pit.

All the bells in England seemed to be peeling in Tamsin's head. She thought she must swoon. To prevent herself from falling she had to hold on to her captor with her gloved hands. From her fingers slipped the reticule, that had belonged to her mother, fashioned out of a large seashell, set in a gilded frame, and the minute silver nosegay holder with its single pink camellia. . . .

All the while she felt the roughness of his beard bruising her chin and neck, his cool, strong fingers caressing the bare flesh of her arms and shoulders, and the dominance of his body against hers.

If I do manage to scream someone must come to my rescue. Desperately she tried to reason with what little sense was still left to her, yet the same thought brought the awareness of what a scandal would be caused. No one—certainly not Aunt Scott and more particularly Sir Everard—would believe in her innocence. No respectable young lady would allow herself to be embraced by any man to whom she was not affianced let alone a complete stranger. No respectable young lady would have been discovered daydreaming unchaperoned in a conservatory. The fact that her solitary state had been Leonie's fault would hardly exonerate her. . . .

Momentarily, one of the man's hands slackened its hold, and Tamsin was able to wrench herself free, the bodice of her gown in some disarray.

It was only then that the somewhat breathless gentleman looked her fully in the face.

As if to ward off a further onslaught Tamsin's hands flew up to cover her bruised mouth from which came

uncontrolled sobbing breaths. Shock made her eyes
even larger and more luminous. As she stared at her
attacker she noted how handsome he was in a perilous
fashion with his dark, curling locks, side-whiskers and
small pointed beard. The formal evening clothes that
were uniform for all gentlemen somehow seemed exotic
on him. She might have taken him for a foreigner—one
of the many pouring into London for the Great Exhibition—or, the devil incarnate.

Her cheeks burned as if she had sat too near an un-
screened fire. There was no trace of the pallor that Aunt
Scott recommended as maidenly and which Leonie concealed by an assiduous application of geranium petals to
her own pale cheeks.

The gentleman's expression gradually altered. Ardour turned to perplexity which in turn gave way to
amusement. He gave a small and unapologetic chuckle.

'Damn me! I fear I mistook you for quite another lady,
my dear little girl.'

Tamsin was astonished to find the pleasant drawling
voice contained no hint of a foreign accent.

'. . . yet I could have sworn I knew that fetching gown
you're wearing . . .' he added as if this explained and
condoned his behaviour.

Aunt Scott had been correct, thought Tamsin dismally, for she had declared white to be more appropriate. If only I had not listened to Leonie who
insisted this rose was so becoming: ' . . . but, darling,
you must wear it,' Tamsin could almost hear the purring
little voice. 'It is even more suited to you than me. No
one apart from us two can know it was mine. I have only
worn it at Baden Baden, and we are unlikely to meet
anyone at the Exhibition Ball whom I met there . . .'

Part of the fault once again lay with Leonie. Then a

sudden realisation shocked Tamsin almost as much as the ardent caresses.

This person—he could not be termed a gentleman—must have mistaken her for Leonie Edgecombe because of the gown, which could only mean they had met in Baden Baden, and had, it would appear, engaged in intimacy greater than conversation; for his had not been a tremulous attempt to steal a kiss from lips untried but the continuation of some previous interlude.

Tamsin was utterly confused. To think that Leonie, who had left London broken-hearted, vowing she could love no one but Mr Elliot James, had actually permitted this stranger to embrace her and thereby risked her reputation and Mr James's love.

'I suppose,' continued the man, smiling but unembarrassed, 'I should ask your pardon,' and his eyes snapped with dark laughter. 'But I cannot regret that which I took so much pleasure in doing and would gladly repeat . . .'

Hastily, Tamsin stepped back into the leafy but less hazardous clutches of the palm fronds. A kind of horrid fascination compelled her to gaze at the stranger. He seemed to emanate some hypnotic power such as she had heard ferrets exert over poor rabbits so that they can the more easily destroy them.

'My dear,' he said easily. 'You must not stare at me with eyes as great as saucers. Surely, you have been taught it is impolite to stare . . .' he grinned ' . . . at strangers. Tidy your gown, for I would not return you to your friends with such ruffled feathers.'

He bent and retrieved the reticule and posy holder, turning them in his hands, as he waited while she rearranged her gown.

Dazedly, Tamsin patted ringlets and headdress, pulled up her bodice to a more modest level and straightened the minute puff sleeves back onto her shoulders. This encounter had turned her sedate world upside down for Aunt Scott's upbringing had never prepared her to meet any man who would treat her other than as a lady of the most genteel experience. No lecture on etiquette had contained advice on how to conduct yourself in these improper circumstances.

'I have no wish to be escorted anywhere,' she said, trying to sound as cold and dignified as a dowager duchess but succeeding only in the breathlessness of a girl just out of the schoolroom.

The man's grin deepened with impudence.

'What! Would you prefer to remain here in these quiet shadows with me? Now, that I call sporting, fair unknown.' He handed back her reticule and a somewhat crushed camellia. 'Might I enquire your name?'

'Certainly not!' Tamsin snapped, horrified, and clutched the belongings against her waist. So long as he did not know whom he had kissed there was no risk of him boasting it abroad. 'I have no wish to remain here with you, or be escorted anywhere by you . . .' As an afterthought she added rather lamely: 'Good evening, sir.'

He did not immediately move yet made no attempt to recapture her. Instead, he contemplated the young girl with an expression which suggested great amusement. At last, he gave a little bow and composed his features into a formal smile.

'May I wish you good evening, fair creature, and hope to have the pleasure of another meeting when we can deepen a friendship begun so auspiciously. I would gladly steal kisses from you until you learned to offer them of your own free will. Then, what delights we might share. Come now, miss, do not look quite so shocked. Did no one ever tell you you were made for love? How very remiss of them.'

Tamsin was too disconcerted to know whether or not he jested.

Reluctantly, he smoothed the white gloves back on to his fine hands and turned. Without retrieving the glass of wine he opened the double doors and left Tamsin standing alone in the conservatory.

It was then that real shock overtook her. She began to tremble. Her teeth chattered as if in the stress of fever. Heat and chill took rapid turns at possessing her flesh, and dried her mouth. She noticed the half-filled glass of champagne, and gulped it down, aware that he must have left it there and that her lips were pressed to the rim at possibly the same place as his had previously been. The wine did little to soothe her agitation. *Pray Heaven we never meet again*, she thought with genuine terror, *so he has no chance of discovering my name. Should anyone ever learn of this I would be quite disgraced.* How Everard Fortune would laugh: for her indiscretion would release him from their arranged marriage. The irksome terms of his papa's last will and testament could be safely set aside so he need not lose his inheritance by refusing to marry her.

Chagrin increased when she allowed herself to realise that far from being the most terrible experience in her whole life the stranger's kisses had been curiously sweet as well as frightening in intensity. Surely, there was something very wrong with her if she could experience any pleasure in so outrageous a situation. Should she not now be lying on the floor in a deep swoon occasioned by shock and disgust?

But, try as she would, Tamsin could not disguise from herself that the kiss and his words had evoked feelings she did not know existed outside poetry and the novels frowned upon by Aunt Scott. Unwillingly, she turned her mind towards Sir Everard Fortune: it was unlikely his embraces, when she had to endure them, would elicit anything save repugnance. Nor could she imagine him telling her that she was made for love.

Tamsin could not refrain from wondering who this person without respect for conventions could be. He had looked and behaved like a brigand or a pirate but such, she presumed, did not possess educated tones or frequent fashionable subscription balls.

The only person who might be able to identify him was Leonie, but Tamsin could scarcely ask her without revealing the reason. Despite their long friendship Miss Edgecombe had given her no hint of a romantic entanglement at Baden Baden, and while Leonie might guard her own secrets jealously Tamsin judged it unwise to trust her with a confidence which could bring about her own ruin even though it would cast little glory upon the good name of Miss Edgecombe.

'You must compose yourself,' Tamsin whispered desperately, 'otherwise someone will surely detect something is amiss and begin to ask questions.'

She laid her face against the chill glass panes in a vain attempt to cool her cheeks and reduce their hectic colour.

Aunt Scott's earlier misgivings about the propriety of attending this Ball had been more than justified although she could never have envisaged the fate that awaited her niece in the conservatory. Only Mrs Edgecombe's eloquent pleading that Tamsin was *so good* for her daughter had compelled Aunt Scott to consent.

While she had doubts as to Miss Edgecombe's bene-

ficial influence on her niece it was difficult to decline
since they were invited to stay at the Edgecombe's
Russell Square house for the duration of the Exhibition
and also to await Sir Everard's eventual arrival.

After all, anyone who was anyone would be in
London for the Exhibition as well as all those who were
nobody in particular, thus presentable lodgings were
expensive and scarce. As Mrs Scott's own home was in
Kent and she could never have afforded a suitable
London establishment for Tamsin's meeting with Sir
Everard, Mrs Edgecombe's generous invitation was an
undisguised blessing.

It was also the cost of attiring her niece fashionably
that had persuaded Aunt Scott to allow her to wear Miss
Edgecombe's cast-offs which had led to consequences
neither she nor Tamsin could have foreseen. As both
young ladies were possessed of similar colouring, most
of Leonie's gowns and bonnets suited Tamsin as admirably as if they had been made for her. Nor did any of the
garments suggest a previous owner for Leonie required a
new bonnet almost as often as the sun rose and she was
not one of those sensible girls (as eulogised by Aunt
Scott) who kept last year's gown for second-best. Not
only were the clothes barely worn but their style was more
frivolous and modish than Aunt Scott would have countenanced had she been footing the dressmaker's bills.

She had never concealed from Tamsin her opinion
that the Edgecombe's patronage was not based on al-
truism. 'They are no doubt delighted that the girl Leonie
befriended at Miss Drew's Young Ladies' Academy in
Tunbridge Wells is to become Lady Fortune. Your marriage could well be instrumental in introducing Mrs
Edgecombe's daughter into a more illustrious social
sphere than would normally be open to her.'

While Tamsin agreed this might be how Mrs Edge-combe viewed the situation, she knew Leonie was too much the harum-scarum to secure the future through social contacts.

It was Miss Edgecombe's very impetuosity that had just imperilled Tamsin's virtue since it had been her idea they leave the ballroom together, ostensibly to smooth their hair and stroll up and down and gossip away from crush and noise. What could be more acceptable—even to Mrs Scott—than the two girls acting as each other's chaperone?

But, once they had gained the conservatory, Tamsin realised Leonie's intentions were quite other than those she had stated to her mamma. Her eyes alight with anticipation, the minx had protested she must step out on to the terrace for a few moments of fresh air but on no account was dear Tamsin to accompany her lest she take cold.

Tamsin was not entirely convinced she would find Leonie alone on the terrace in the rain or out there at all. For, although nothing had been said, she could not doubt some tryst had been arranged with Mr Elliot James. Since the couple had not met for over three months there was more for them to say to each other than might be contained in a few moments. While personal contact may have been impossible, Tamsin felt sure letters had passed between Leonie and Mr James, one of which had probably arranged this evening's rendezvous.

It was all due to Mr James that Leonie had been sent to the healthy distractions of Baden Baden to stay with distant cousins. Mrs Edgecombe had been convinced that fashionable spa would help her daughter forget her undesirable attachment to the penniless drawing master.

However, Tamsin knew Leonie well enough to deduce her mamma's object had not been achieved. Whatever embraces she might now suspect Leonie had exchanged with another there was as yet no reason to assume anyone had seriously replaced Mr James in Miss Edgecombe's affections.

Now, many more moments than a few had elapsed since they had quit the ballroom but Tamsin was still unable to return to her aunt and Mrs Edgecombe without revealing Leonie's absence or how she had apparently been by herself for so long. Besides, she dreaded re-entering that ballroom in case that gentleman, most importunately, sought to be introduced to her. In such an unspeakable event her distress must make the world and Aunt Scott ask questions Tamsin would prefer not to answer.

Why, oh why need Leonie always behave in such a rash manner which must not only bring scandal upon herself but would this time also deliver her friend into the valley of humiliation?

When, a few minutes later, Aunt Scott and Mrs Edgecombe hurried into the conservatory, Tamsin learned with relief that at least she would not have to return to the ballroom. Her absence remained unquestioned and her agitation unmarked, for a greater humiliation had occurred which must abruptly bring to an end their presence at the Exhibition Ball.

It seemed Mrs Edgecombe had just received a message from her daughter explaining how Leonie had suddenly felt unwell and in order not to spoil Tamsin's evening had chosen to go home in a hansom cab.

'Oh, the shame of it!' moaned Mrs Edgecombe, crushing the feathers on her fan with nervous fingers. 'Alone in a hansom . . .'

'Greater the shame,' insisted Aunt Scott with grim logic, 'if she is not alone in the cab.'

Tamsin was required to say nothing. She was quite convinced Leonie had an escort on her homeward journey. Just how long it would be before Mrs Edgecombe and Aunt Scott discovered that was open to speculation. At least, Leonie's recklessness shielded her own anxiety from attracting comment. It could only be presumed Miss Lucas's extreme perturbation was caused by her friend's flagrant behaviour . . .

CHAPTER
TWO

IT was scarcely dawn when Tamsin awoke.

She lay against the downy pillows wondering at the joyous clamour of the bells. It could not be Sunday. Only then did she recall how today, Thursday, 1st May, all London's church bells were to be rung to celebrate the opening of the Great Exhibition of the Works of Industry of all Nations by Her Gracious Majesty, Queen Victoria.

The day Tamsin and all London had looked forward to had finally arrived.

She climbed out of the half tester bed to kneel on the window seat and peep through the heavy curtains, aware that Aunt Scott would have condemned a nightgown as indecorous attire for window-gazing, even at that hour. How disappointing it was to see a steady drizzle sheening the empty square. At least, there were some gaps in the clouds which hinted the weather might clear. If she were to wear Leonie's beautiful, but discarded, blue and green shot taffeta gown for the opening it would be a pity for the scalloped and silk-braided hem to be damp spotted.

Only a few days before Tamsin and Leonie had been overjoyed to learn they could go to the royal opening. Originally, it was to have been a private occasion, but that doyen of respectable public opinion, *The Times*, had observed tartly how Queen Victoria was not Lady Godiva and it was unfair that the twenty-five thousand people who had paid out three guineas (in the case of gentlemen) and two guineas (in the case of ladies) for their season tickets should be denied the opportunity of attending the Great Exhibition's gala opening.

Public opinion—not to say commonsense—had triumphed.

Aunt Scott's disapproval of the 'Thunderer's' mention of the Queen and Lady Godiva on the same page had almost induced her to wonder if it would be more proper *not* to attend the opening. To Tamsin's relief, Mrs Edgecombe's persuasion had prevailed: she had most sensibly pointed out what a waste of two guineas it would be not to take full advantage of all that the tickets afforded. Besides, the chance to go amongst such glittering company did not occur every day.

Of course, like all London, high and low, Tamsin and Aunt Scott had accompanied the Edgecombes to Hyde Park almost daily to marvel at the progress of Mr Paxton's glass edifice which had taken some twenty-two weeks to erect. Aunt Scott might have deemed such curiosity vulgar had not the Queen and her family regularly visited the site to marvel at the building Punch had so aptly dubbed the 'Crystal Palace'.

As the fantastic structure grew so did speculation as to its eventual exhibits until Tamsin found herself wishing away the days until she could visit this crystal palace of splendours, almost heedless that the passage of time must also bring her closer to Sir Everard Fortune.

Had anyone suggested to Tamsin her interest in the Exhibition that Prince Albert had so skilfully organised might be supplanted by another event she would not have believed it. Yet, to her astonishment and bewilderment, even the Great Exhibition seemed slightly pedestrian beside the previous evening's events. That unnamed man would not let her forget him however much she strove to banish him from her mind, and he elbowed out of the way all the small usual thoughts.

She had slept but little, for each time she closed her eyes the stranger was waiting for her, his dark eyes mocking her discomfiture. In dreams, his arms and lips pursued her until she feared to sleep. Yet she was compelled to admit to her innermost self that these dreams were not as wholly disagreeable as those she sometimes had about Sir Everard.

It seemed odd—not to say shocking—that in sleep she had no control over her mind. Had Aunt Scott known of this she would have insisted it demonstrated her niece's moral turpitude.

A faint tap at the door heralded a barefoot Leonie in her nightgown, her face pale and framed by a heavy shawl of unplaited hair. She curled herself under the counterpane on Tamsin's bed before asking:

'I trust I am not disturbing you, dearest, but I just could not sleep. Mamma gave me such a frightful lecture last night that my poor head quite aches.'

Tamsin had heard nothing of the lengthy conversation between mother and daughter which took place behind the closed doors of Leonie's bedroom. Anyway as soon as they arrived home from the Ball Aunt Scott delivered a homily on how damaging the behaviour of certain young females could be to their friends. Sir Everard might regard Tamsin as guilty by association which made it doubly important that her own behaviour should resemble that of Caesar's wife.

It seemed to Tamsin that Caesar's wife must have led a very dull life indeed; only she was too much in awe of her aunt to mention this.

'Well, it was rather foolish of you to leave the ball like

that,' Tamsin chided gently. 'You must have realised how anxious your mamma would be.'

Leonie's lips puckered crossly. 'Dearest, don't scold. It was a most dreary ball, was it not? Nothing exciting happened.'

Fortunately, she was examining her gleaming finger-nails as she spoke, and so did not see the colour suffuse Tamsin's face and neck.

'You seemed to have little difficulty in finding part-ners,' Tamsin observed.

'Oh, they were so boring. I promise you, you miss nothing by not being allowed to dance. I am sure *your* Sir Everard will prove vastly more amusing than any of those boring fellows.'

Tamsin ignored this reference to Everard Fortune for she knew Leonie considered him a most alluring person-age and was quite unable to comprehend her own aver-sion for the gentleman society rumour-mongers re-garded as a rich seam of material. His penchants for gaming and the society of actresses, artists and other Bohemians, were widely known and discussed until it was impossible to decide where truth ended and gossip began. However, his choice to live abroad for so many years while his roots and future lay in England convinced the malicious that by now his habits and manners were too depraved for re-entry into polite society . . . like the late Lord Byron who at least had the doubtful excuse of a club foot and being a poet.

'And did you go home all alone?'

Leonie tried to look solemn, but the glint in her eyes denied an inner gravity. 'I fear I did not. Pray, do not tell Mamma, for I fibbed to her. Anyway, don't you consider it more proper for me to have been escorted?'

Even before she spoke them Tamsin realised her

words were futile: 'Mrs Edgecombe desires only what is good for you.'

'And so do I,' retorted the unrepentant daughter.

'But, perhaps she knows best. Was your escort Mr James?'

'Of course. Whom else?' Leonie sounded quite shocked that it might be thought she would hazard her reputation by being alone with any gentleman other than the true object of her affections. Her talent at duplicity left Tamsin quite breathless: she doubted she could ever learn a similar skill.

'Your mamma will have guessed as much. No wonder she is so distressed, having forbidden you ever again to see Mr James.'

'I shall do more than see him again. I intend to become his wife.'

'Mrs Edgecombe will never give you her permission.'

'We can always elope.'

Tamsin was astounded that Leonie could propose such a wild scheme with no more trepidation than if she had suggested a stroll in the square.

'But, the scandal . . .'

'Fiddlesticks to scandal! Once we are married, who is going to gossip?' Leonie giggled. 'Dearest, you begin to sound like your worthy aunt whose favourite maxim is "duty is there to be done" which she never ceases telling Mamma is what she made you embroider on your first sampler when you were five and came to live with her. Are you going to remind me of my duty? You must not behave so primly with Sir Everard or he will grow bored.'

'And if I do not behave so primly,' Tamsin said ruefully, 'Aunt Scott insists Everard will use that as a pretext to escape our marriage. Rumour early reached our ears of how he seeks to discover something not quite proper about me which will persuade the Fortune family lawyers as to my undesirability as a wife, even while he forges himself a reputation as a rake without any qualms of this being made known to me. Aunt Scott thinks Everard is quite capable of manufacturing some scandal to discredit me, which makes her all the more vigilant of my behaviour. However much she deplores his character and that our union is governed by the ridiculous wills drawn up by two cup-shot papas, who passed away before recognising the folly of their schemes, Aunt Scott holds it as her sacred duty to ensure I marry Everard Fortune.'

Tamsin's laughter had a bitter ring to it. 'Do you realise my whole life has been governed by what would please or displease Everard? It is the method by which Aunt Scott has exacted my complete obedience these last thirteen years. I can do nothing—be it wave at you from my window, play too heartily upon the pianoforte, or fail to sit up backboard straight—in case Everard learn of it on his peregrinations around Europe and be aggrieved. I assure you, Leonie, it is excessively difficult to wish to please someone of whom I have only the worst recollections.'

Leonie shook her head, unsure of how best to offer Tamsin some words of comfort. Besides, her own affairs were uppermost in her thoughts. 'But, don't you think it would be vastly romantic to steal away one night and go abroad to marry?' she persisted. Her expression grew more earnest. 'I do wonder what I should wear for the journey . . .'

Romantic certainly, thought Tamsin, but scarcely practical. How like Leonie to consider her appearance even at such a time.

'Has Mr James suggested as much?' she asked.

Leonie shook back her cape of hair. 'No, he is far too cautious. He talks about how poor we shall be if we marry now and wants to wait until his reputation as an artist is established. Besides, he would like us to have Mamma's blessing. I told him I do not care *this* for money.'

'This' was a snap of her childlike fingers.

Tamsin considered it more diplomatic not to point out that while Leonie might not care about money she manifestly cared about what could be bought with it. She just could not envisage her extravagant friend scrimping and saving and living on a diet of love and penury.

'What about the dowry your papa left in trust for you?' How Tamsin wished Mr Lucas had made a similar sensible provision for her future so that she need not depend on marriage to Everard for her sole security.

Of course, dear papa had only intended the best for her, wanting his little girl to have wealth and title, especially as he had even managed to gamble away to Sir Oliver Fortune that small portion left to her as a dowry by her sweet mamma who died in giving her life. He could not have realised his will, which bequeathed her nothing but debts and recommended she marry Everard Fortune as soon after her eighteenth birthday as possible, had shackled her to a man she loathed who reciprocated her feelings.

Being the closest of cronies, Mr Roger Lucas and Sir Oliver Fortune had entertained no doubts that their offspring were made for each other. They had been enthusiastic about uniting their two names, convinced their children, as well as their descendants, must inherit the tender graces and virtues of the two late mammas (who had also been the best of friends) devoid of any trace of their own somewhat rapscallion characteristics.

It had been a sad fact neither gentleman was prepared to accept that Everard at fourteen and Tamsin at four appeared to agree like cat and dog! It did not bode a happy-ever-after future. Wisely, the fond, but blinkered papas, had decreed the children should not meet again until Tamsin was a young lady of eighteen; that measure they were convinced would prevent any childish antipathy from developing.

The scheme had not proved a success.

'Absence makes the heart grow fond' may have been an adage Tamsin could neatly embroider and surround with fat red hearts and vivid flowers, but it was one she found harder to accept. She liked Everard no better for not having seen nor heard from him these fourteen years. Manifestly, he was not overly anxious to resume their acquaintanceship, for her eighteenth birthday had come and gone these six months before turgid word came from the Fortune family lawyers that Sir Everard might shortly be returning to English soil. Tamsin grimly deduced his motive to be financial embarrassment rather than any romantic attachment.

While her eyes darkened to slate with angry thoughts of Everard Fortune Leonie's were no less wrathful. 'Mamma said the trustees will never release any of that dowry unless they approve my choice of husband.' Her indignation exploded. 'She vows Mr James is the kind who is only interested in laying his hands on a comfortable dowry and uses his skill as drawing-master to enter the homes of the well-to-do where there are marriageable daughters.'

She clasped her hands imploringly: 'But you know he is not like that, Tamsin, don't you? You don't think he is a fortune-hunter . . .'

Tamsin smiled slightly. 'Dearest, if anyone is a fortune-hunter, then I am, if you will excuse the pun, although I am forced to hunt a Fortune I should prefer not to catch.'

Leonie laughed delightedly and clapped her hands. 'But you do think Elliot is fine and honourable, don't you?' she insisted.

Tamsin did not know. She had encountered the pleasant-faced young man only twice on previous visits to the Edgecombe house before Mrs Edgecombe became suspicious of her daughter's enthusiasm for drawing lessons and her instructor. To Tamsin, Mr James had seemed shy and respectful, almost eclipsed by Leonie's ebullience. Even to her inexperienced eyes it was obvious Miss Edgecombe was his goddess and she thought it must be delightful to be the centre of a gentleman's universe, but doubted it was a position she would occupy in Sir Everard's.

But, had Mr James, she wondered idly, told Leonie she was made for love? That was a question she dared not put, and indeed an invasion into her thoughts made her blush with embarrassment.

Only when Leonie had recounted whom Tamsin was to marry did Mr James volunteer somewhat hesitantly: 'Oh, I met Sir Everard Fortune in Paris at a friend's studio. He was kind enough to admire some of my works. He takes a great interest in modern artists.'

Leonie had interrupted her admirer saucily: 'And their models too, I daresay, if half what we hear of him is true, is that not so?'

Mr James's smooth cheeks had grown alarmingly pink.

'Is he really so wicked?' Leonie had continued her interrogation.

'He seemed a pleasant enough gentleman,' was all Mr James would say, and it was impossible to decide whether this was his honest opinion or if he wished to spare Miss Lucas's feelings.

Leonie had pouted with disappointment. 'How absurdly dull. I hoped you would recount some shocking misdeed,' and she laughed naughtily. 'But, of course, in the face of our combined feminine curiosity, you gentlemen always stick together. I suppose Sir Everard would describe you as *a pleasant enough gentleman*,' and she mimicked her teacher's tone, 'even if he knew you'd been up to some wickedness.'

In vain, did a flustered Mr James protest he had committed no great indiscretion in Paris, or elsewhere, but Leonie refused to be convinced. Indeed, Tamsin understood her well enough to know she would have preferred his reputation to be more audacious. She wondered if Leonie would dote on Mr James quite so much were he not forbidden fruit. Even as a schoolgirl Leonie had favoured adventure to everyday life and had been warned by her teachers it would lead her into troubled waters.

'He seems an upright person,' Tamsin admitted slowly. 'But have we experience enough to judge whether what we see is the truth or merely a vizard concealing the truth?' And she was alarmed to realise that she was not considering Mr James as she spoke but that impudent stranger in the conservatory.

The arrival of Minnie bearing a large copper jug of hot water prevented Leonie from responding.

Tamsin poured some of the steaming water into her blue and white wash bowl and began to sponge her face. In a voice slightly muffled by a flannel she said: 'If we are to reach the Exhibition in good time we ought to start getting ready . . .'

Leonie yawned and stretched like a kitten but made no move to leave her comfortable nest. 'Mamma has forbidden me to go. That is my punishment for last night. And she has decided not to go either for she says she is too ashamed of me to be seen in public today, but I suspect she prefers to stay at home and keep an eye on me.'

Tamsin turned a sympathetic face towards her. 'How terrible. I am so sorry.'

Leonie shrugged. 'Since I have a season ticket and the Exhibition continues until October there will be many chances to visit it. Far more provoking is that tomorrow I am to go to Gloucestershire to stay at my Uncle Septimus's rectory. A most boring man who will look with disapproval at my gowns and bonnets and deliver daily sermons on the virtue of obedience and the folly of vanity. If he did not already have a wife of similar qualities in Aunt Sophronia I should suggest we introduce him to your aunt.' She giggled at the idea. 'Mamma insists her brother will persuade me against my fondness for Mr James.'

'You cannot very well gainsay your mother and your uncle,' said Tamsin doubtfully.

Leonie blew delicately as if Tamsin's words were so many dandelion clocks that would collapse and drift away on the breeze. 'I can and I will. I must send word to my dear Elliot explaining my sudden banishment. He must arrange to come to Gloucestershire too, where I am sure we will be able to meet secretly.'

'As you managed yesterday evening. Who acts as your go-between?'

A dimple appeared in Leonie's pointed chin. 'Minnie. She has a most romantic nature. Besides, I know her to

have a follower. The post boy. If Mamma were to discover she would lose her place, so in exchange for my
silence Minnie runs these confidential little errands for
me.'

'She will lose her place if ever Mrs Edgecombe does
discover how she abets you,' Tamsin pointed out
soberly. 'Are you being quite fair to poor Minnie?'

'Hoity-toity, Miss Virtue?' snapped Leonie. She did
not like to be told she was in the wrong. 'It is all very well
for you to be so nice when you do not know what it is to
be in love. If ever it should happen to you I doubt you
will behave quite as decorously as your aunt
recommends.'

Tamsin bit her lips. 'I fear that it is a situation I shall
never explore,' and her voice trembled slightly.

Immediately Leonie was contrite. 'Do not be so
downcast, dearest. I did not intend to be harsh. I am sure
you will be blissfully happy with Sir Everard despite your
present doubts, and he will fall in love with you the
minute he sets eyes on your sweet face.' Hurriedly, she
added: 'You must borrow the new bonnet I had planned
to wear today. The capote's dark green ribbons will
match the trimming on your gown. Be sure to tie them to
a side for that is a more fetching style than a bow directly
beneath the chin.'

However tiresome Leonie might find it to be opposed
she did not like to be thought unkind, and indeed had
sweetened her hold on Minnie with small gifts of pins
and ribbons.

'Dear Leonie, how generous you always are to me.'

Leonie kissed her finger tips in a disclaiming gesture.

'You are welcome to the bonnet. I shall not need it
today. Because of the Exhibition's opening most of the
shops are closed, and I presume Mamma will forbid me

leaving the house for any reason. It is a pleasure to see you handsomely rigged out after those atrocious gowns of serge and gingham provided by your aunt. She appears to equate virtue with dowdiness.' Leonie chuckled. 'I expect being dowdy helps one to be good . . .

'One day, when you are Lady Fortune, perhaps you will recall my small kindnesses and lend Mrs James— poor as the proverbial churchmouse—your parure of diamonds or your collar of emeralds or whatever other priceless trinkets Sir Everard bestows upon his bride.'

'From what I know of him,' Tamsin retorted, remembering his refusal even to let her play with the hoop he had long outgrown, 'he is unlikely to present me with anything.'

'But there are the Fortune jewels. His Mamma was wealthy in her own right and possessed costly gems in some abundance and it is said Sir Oliver lavished even more splendid ones upon her. All those baubles will be Everard's when he marries you.'

It had never ceased to astonish Tamsin that Leonie knew more about the Fortune possessions than she did, partly from natural curiosity and partly because one of the Fortune estates, Stillwater, was only a few miles away from Mrs Edgecombe's brother's rectory at Fairford. Leonie's infrequent visits to her uncle were always spiced with local gossip about the misdeeds of the heir to Stillwater, made all the more intriguing because he had not visited the place in years.

Miss Edgecombe was entranced by what she considered Tamsim's romantic prospects. Why, it was better than any French novel which she read unbeknown to her Mamma. Privately, she thought herself more suited for such a thrilling alliance than Tamsin who seemed too goody-good for one of Sir Everard's kidney. In Leonie's opinion fate had been most provoking in selecting the wrong girl to be Lady Fortune.

'How sorry I was to leave Baden Baden before Sir Everard's arrival. Everyone was discussing his amorous exploits.' Tamsin had heard Leonie express these regrets at least a dozen times since her return to London. 'He sounds very wicked . . . and delightful. In order to introduce myself to him I should have taken advantage of *our friendship*, dearest, as well as reminding him that my uncle is a neighbour of his. Then, I could have told you what he is really like, and you would not have to rely on all those silly stories about him. I have always thought it a pity he never visited Stillwater while I was staying with Uncle Septimus for I would most assuredly have made his acquaintance.'

She did not voice her daydream of Sir Everard being so bewitched by her that he would have cast Tamsin aside—although how then he could have secured his late papa's wealth she could not resolve.

'To judge by what we have heard of his manners your precocity on whatever pretext might have been ill-advised,' Tamsin observed drily, unaware of Leonie's fantasies.

With sweeping strokes of the tortoiseshell-backed brush she began to smooth her light brown hair. Only when the tresses concealed her face did she remark: 'I am certain Baden Baden offered more interesting distractions than the imminent arrival of Sir Everard,' and she was mortified to feel her cheeks begin to burn.

'Perhaps,' Leonie said airily. 'But now I am reunited with my dear James I wonder at thinking any gentleman of interest.'

Leonie's apparent indifference did not help Tamsin to

probe further. She was disconcerted to realise her own relief at Miss Edgecombe's forgetfulness of one with whom she must have been on the closest of terms. . . .

Normally, breakfast at the Edgecombe's was a lavish and cheerful affair where plans for the day ahead were discussed and the previous evening's entertainment reviewed. This morning, however, Leonie's latest indiscretion cast gloom on the silver tea kettle and even seemed to mute the tantalizing aromas wafting from the several covered hot dishes on the side table. Uneasy silence rather than amiable chatter filled the dining-room.

Poor Mrs Edgecombe, usually pink and placid, in flounced morning gown and ribboned cap, was quite pale and nervous, and invited Mrs Scott to preside over the household prayers in her stead.

This was a duty that Tamsin's aunt accepted glady, and under her tutelage the usual brief sentence of gratitude for their daily food became a long and convoluted prayer that all within the house should learn duty and show obedience.

Tamsin could hear the crackle of starched aprons and printed gowns as the maids clustered in the doorway fidgeted uneasily, anxious to begin cleaning the bedrooms. Despite a meekly bowed head, Leonie's fingers twitched irritably at the edge of her lace bertha, conscious that most of Mrs Scott's words were directed towards her. A sharp rap at the street door announced the arrival of the post and coincided with Aunt Scott's lugubrious 'Amen'.

Much relieved the maids scurried away to leave the occupants of the dining-room to break their fast. Neither Mrs Edgecombe nor her daughter had much appetite: the former toyed with a muffin while the latter picked sulkily at a sliver of cold ham.

Although Mrs Edgecombe had filled her plate with a plentiful selection of scrambled eggs, kidneys, bacon and fish, Tamsin found it hard to swallow even the smallest morsel. Memory of the evening's events seemed to produce a nervous lump in her throat and she felt guiltily grateful that Leonie's disgrace was occupying her aunt's attention so that she did not seek to discover the cause of her niece's agitation.

All Tamsin could do to reassure herself was to reason that in so large a place as London it was unlikely she would ever again encounter that gentleman and he would have no opportunity of discovering her name even if such as he would care to know it.

Only Aunt Scott's appetite was in no way blunted. She held it to be her duty to eat all that was set before her, and it was a duty she performed zealously.

'Do try to eat a little, Tamsin, my dear,' Mrs Edgecombe urged gently. 'You are so pale this morning. I fear none of us slept much last night.' She cast a reproachful glance at Leonie, 'But if you are to enjoy your day you will need all your strength.'

'Oh, that is the way Tamsin keeps her waist at less than nineteen inches,' said Leonie a trifle enviously, for it must be admitted that all the gowns she passed to Tamsin had needed to be taken in.

'Young ladies should not appear to eat excessively,' Aunt Scott declared, helping herself to another portion of fish. 'Gentlemen prefer 'em to be fragile with the appetite of a butterfly.'

Mrs Edgecombe tittered behind her hand. 'Ah, but we have our ways round that little problem, do we not, dear Mrs Scott? Leonie and I always eat well *before* we go anywhere so that our appetites appear delicate. It is not refined to see a girl gorging herself in public however choice the viands.'

Her mouth a little too full for a verbal response, Mrs Scott nodded vigorously in agreement.

'Imagine when you are Lady Fortune, Tamsin,' Leonie said covetously. 'You may lie abed for as long as you choose, and have your maid bring trays of hot chocolate and fine cakes and peaches and strawberries from your own hot houses. You will not need to be dressed before eleven o'clock, and . . .'

Mrs Scott regarded this as a very indelicate topic, and interrupted acidly: 'Miss Edgecombe, no niece of mine will lead such an idle life. I have taught Thomasina that she must rise two hours after the servants, and be dressed and coiffed for the day ahead. Then she must ascertain all is cleaned and polished and the fires lit before breakfast is served. An indolent mistress deserves and gets feckless servants.'

Leonie was not easily rebuked and muttered sullenly: 'That is to keep a dog and bark yourself.'

Mrs Edgecombe reproved her daughter mildly: 'Well, my dear, I think it is time you paid more attention to domestic duties. Perhaps I have allowed you too much freedom which is why your head is filled with nothing but fashion and foolishness. Today, you will help me check the linen and silver cupboards as I do each month. Then we shall ask cook to give us an account of what jams and pickles are left from the winter so that when we begin bottling and preserving we may know just how much is required.'

'And Thomasina will lend Miss Edgecombe her household album,' volunteered Aunt Scott helpfully. 'I have encouraged her to keep one since her twelfth birthday, and now she has a most useful collection of receipts.

There is one for furniture polish which I particularly
recommend, and a remedy for the ague which cannot be
bettered. No matter how fortunate a position a lady finds
herself in after marriage she must understand exactly
how to manage her home so that she can successfully
command others.'

'Oh, I do agree,' said Mrs Edgecombe, for she considered Mrs Scott a paragon of all the virtues, albeit a
fierce one. She smiled encouragingly at her daughter.
'Leonie, you may spend this afternoon copying them
out. Do not look so glum, dear girl, one day when you
are mistress of your own household you will be glad of
such hints.'

Leonie's expression suggested anything but gratitude,
but she was spared any more advice by the arrival of a
rather breathless pink-cheeked Minnie. Beneath the
muslin cap the maid's eyes were as bright as a robin's.
On a salver she carried a letter. She bobbed a curtsy and
addressed her mistress: 'Please, ma'am, the post has just
arrived. This one is for Mrs Scott.'

The recipient of the letter stared suspiciously at Minnie's departing back. From experience Tamsin knew
that had this been her house her aunt would have immediately sniffed out the presence of a follower and
taken the appropriate action. Mrs Scott glowered at the
letter as if it had committed an act of impropriety by
arriving while she was crunching toast, and she drank
some tea before opening it. As she perused its contents
her expression grew more forbidding.

'Not bad news, ma'am?' Mrs Edgecombe asked. Concern as well as curiosity tinged her question.

'That man!' snorted Aunt Scott. 'As I always say: like
father like son!'

Tamsin's heart lurched heavily, for her aunt employed

that phrase to refer only to one person.

'Is it from Sir Everard?' cried Leonie, forgetting she had intended to appear demure and chastened. 'When is he coming to claim Tamsin? Oh, Mrs Scott, do tell us.'

'No, miss, it is not from Sir Everard Fortune,' snapped Mrs Scott, glaring at Miss Edgecombe with distaste. Inwardly, she admitted that even if she had that girl in her charge for the next twenty years she could not cure her wilfulness.

Tamsin knew better than to voice her own curiosity. She had learned that given time her aunt would always communicate a confidence.

As if the two girls were not present, Mrs Scott turned confidentially to Mrs Edgecombe: 'It is from Mr Graveny of Graveny and Hampden—a most eminent and respectable firm of lawyers who handle all the Fortune affairs as well as the trifling ones of my late brother. He writes that Sir Everard Fortune is delayed in France . . .' She sniffed contemptuously, '. . . whatever that means. He is sending as his envoy a certain Mr . . .' she re-read the name, 'David St John who is a distant cousin. He will call on us tomorrow at three bearing a letter from Sir Everard and the engagement ring.'

Tamsin felt suddenly quite faint. She had always hoped that some mysterious fate might intervene, but now nothing could prevent this odious marriage from taking place. No doubt Mr St John was as despicable as his cousin. That Sir Everard had chosen to send the betrothal ring and the first letter he had ever penned to her by this stranger proclaimed to the world his reluctance to wed Miss Lucas and that he was only doing so because of his father's will.

'It is certainly a curious way of paying court to your future wife,' observed Leonie, expressing aloud what everybody else at the table was thinking privately. 'He does not seem in a great hurry to be reunited with you, Tamsin dearest, does he?'

'I am sure Sir Everard's reasons for the delay are excellent,' said Mrs Edgecombe kindly, reproachfully shaking her head at her daughter. 'That he sends his cousin ahead with the ring shows he does not intend to postpone matters any longer than necessary.'

Leonie tossed her head so that the ringlets bounced against her cheeks. She gave a small superior smile. Her own dear Mr James might not be titled or potentially wealthy but at least she was certain of his affection for her.

'It is quite unfair that this Mr St John comes to-morrow,' she remarked peevishly, 'for I shall not be here to meet him. I should like to inspect your ring, Tamsin, and discover if the cousin is as dashing as Sir Everard is said to be . . .'

Her customary patience set aside, Mrs Edgecombe turned sharply on her daughter: 'Well, my dear, I am pleased you will be absent, for I do not want word to get back to Sir Everard Fortune that my daughter is a flighty, disobedient female, or else he might consider you quite an unsuitable friend for his future wife.'

Leonie's bottom lip pouted mutinously and her eyes glittered with angry tears.

Tactfully, Tamsin interposed: 'There will be plenty of opportunity for you to see the ring, Leonie, and I am sure you will meet Mr St John in due course.'

Her serene tone was a triumph of her aunt's training in self-control and gave no hint of the churning inner misery and commanded even Miss Edgecombe's gape-mouthed amazement.

'I think you should put on your bonnets,' suggested

Mrs Edgecombe, 'for I fear there will be a great crush on the route to Hyde Park and I do not want you to miss one minute of the spectacle so you may recount it all to us.'

Their early start proved sensible for by ten o'clock the traffic in Oxford Street was as thick as the best chutney. The Edgecombe carriage had to squeeze its way among countless other equipages as well as the many horse-drawn omnibuses with folk literally clinging on to their roofs.

Never had Tamsin seen the streets so crowded or the crowds so good-humoured. Her spirits refused to remain crushed and she began to smile. If the rest of my days are to be spent regretting my marriage then I must enjoy every moment until then, she vowed silently to herself.

Nobody could doubt where all London was heading. Every omnibus bore on its side a placard with the legend 'To the Exhibition'. Not only was everyone arrayed in their best finery but the horses had new reins and rosettes, and more rosettes and streamers adorned the coats and whips of drivers.

In celebration Mrs Scott permitted herself a faint smile. Tamsin would have been astonished to know her aunt was in fact feeling rather pleased with her. Thomasina seemed to have turned out to be the perfect little lady, quiet and submissive, skilled in all those gentle arts which befitted her station. Perhaps a shade too pretty, but that is her mamma's blood, conceded Mrs Scott indulgently, for she had been very fond of Isobel Lucas and had never made any secret that she thought her far too good for her scapegrace brother. Thank Heaven, her niece showed no sign of her papa's nature. Roger had always been a problem. No, she was content: Thomasina was predictable and would never give her cause to worry.

Only one factor saddened Mrs Scott, but there was no help against it: that her niece must marry this blackguard who demonstrably had not the slightest affection for her, would never recognise her virtues, and would no doubt lead her a most unhappy dance. That was Roger's fault. Had he not been so profligate with what money he had he would never have been tempted into drawing up such a ridiculous will or agreeing to the even more ludicrous terms contained in Sir Oliver's.

'How I should like to ride in an omnibus,' Tamsin ventured. 'Leonie has travelled on them several times.'

'Nothing Miss Edgecombe has done or will do surprises me,' retorted Mrs Scott, who believed Leonie capable of anything shocking including donning that unladylike costume created by the American woman, Amelia Bloomer. 'But I do not consider it a very genteel way of going around town. Just look at those shameless creatures up there.'

Tamsin followed her aunt's kid-gloved finger to see a bevy of girls escorted by some very young gentlemen squeezed close together on the long knifeboard seats on the top of an omnibus. Judging by their laughter they were having a very good time. Even the intermittent showers did not dampen their good humour for all it draggled their bonnets. Tamsin felt a tug of envy for a lighthearted freedom she had never experienced.

'If that "decency board" was not placed in front,' Aunt Scott whispered, although it was doubtful the Edgecombe coachman could have heard her scream above the traffic's din, 'you might glimpse their ankles. I doubt the day will ever come when real ladies ride on top of such vehicles.' With an unusual burst of enthusiasm she confessed: 'If I were to use an omnibus I should choose the Franklinski. It is more refined,' she nodded her head towards an omnibus with the peculiar feature that each passenger on both levels had an individual compartment and could communicate with the driver through a separate speaking tube. 'That way one does not have to mix with the vulgar herd or attract the attentions of pickpockets, who I am sure are having a profitable day.'

By the time they reached the park the sun was trying to emerge. Tamsin could scarcely believe the scene her eyes showed her. 'I've never seen so many people, aunt. How many do you suppose are here?'

Only afterwards could the newspaper give her the answer: approximately half a million.

Tha tall trees were almost hidden by countless youths and small boys who had climbed up to gain a better vantage point. Although soaking, the grass was covered with families of picnickers, many of whom must have been there the entire night. To the popular strains of military bands groups of men and girls were actually dancing where there was sufficient space, and Rotten Row was only kept clear by the assiduous efforts of top-hatted constables.

Clearly, all those who were not fortunate enough to afford season tickets were still intent on enjoying the opening of the Exhibition.

'I fear some of them are intoxicated,' Aunt Scott remarked. 'How relieved I am that none of the refreshment rooms at the Exhibition will serve anything but the lightest of beverages. It would be fatal to have inebriates staggering around an edifice composed of glass.'

In the watery sunlight the building was indeed a palace of crystal, a sight from a fairytale. Above it fluttered flags of all nations announcing that this was to be an international exhibition of industry.

'It will probably splinter and cut us all to shreds when the royal salute is fired,' predicted Mrs Scott gloomily, while she and Tamsin waited their turn to reach the entrance. 'I do hope Mr Paxton knew what he was about building it in glass. After all, he was only a gardener to begin with.'

'Oh aunt,' Tamsin protested laughing. 'Mr Paxton's design is much esteemed by the Duke of Devonshire for whom he worked, and many others, including,' she added slyly, 'the Duke of Wellington.' For she knew the Duke was not only a national hero but one approved of by Aunt Scott.

'I suppose it must be all right if *he* thinks so.'

At the southern entrance their conversation waned. Like everyone else they could only gasp and admire this modern wonder of the world. A mighty elm tree soared through the glass roof to fan itself across the southern arch.

'It was his grace's clever notion to introduce sparrow-hawks to clear the trees within the building of sparrows which were causing . . . ahem . . . damage to exhibits and decorations,' whispered Mrs Scott. She added somewhat unnecessarily: 'It would have been most un-wise to attempt to shoot the birds down in here.'

Bordering the long transept were statues, tropical plants and banks of flowers. Behind the red carpets were rows of small chairs provided for the ladies. Where nave and transept crossed sparkled the great cut-glass water-fall. As the water played beneath the light it seemed to toss myriad diamond flecks into the air.

Beyond, in the northern transept, was the dais on which stood the Chair of State under a canopy of blue satin.

In contrast to the sombre apparel of the gentlemen the

ladies' gowns and shawls seemed even more vibrant so that the main hall and galleries resembled a vast hot house of fantastic blooms. That many of the foreign exhibits in the Eastern part of the building were still in confusion was obscured by the host of people.

As Tamsin and Aunt Scott took their places they, like everyone around, were captivated by the arrival of a Chinese mandarin with a very long pigtail: a figure neither of them quite believed existed outside illustrated volumes on distant lands. The spattering of rain against the glass roof high above went almost unnoticed for it was drowned by a sudden burst of cheering, in which Aunt Scott unreservedly joined, at the appearance of the Duke of Wellington, and it was whispered that today was the noble old gentleman's eighty-second birthday. Everyone was hugely entertained when the mandarin greeted the duke with a deep bow.

Just before midday the sun re-emerged to produce suitably royal weather. A salute of guns announced the monarch's arrival. Tamsin was much relieved her aunt's prediction had proved incorrect.

To a flourish of trumpets the royal procession entered through the immense bronze gates at the end of the northern transept.

It was the first time Tamsin had ever seen the Queen in real life: Her Majesty was quite beautiful in a gown of pink and silver with a headdress of diamonds and ostrich feathers, and she was clearly delighted with everything she saw and immensely proud of her husband's role in organizing this Great Exhibition. Prince Albert proved to be a most handsome and distinguished figure in his Field-Marshal's uniform, and Tamsin thought the royal children quite adorable, especially the Prince of Wales, dressed in a kilt.

The waves of cheering that greeted the queen were so resounding they seemed almost to threaten to crack the glass building. But even greater was the sound produced by the sonorous tones of organ music and a thousand voices swelling to sing the National Anthem.

After the royal speeches—Aunt Scott and Tamsin were agreed that Her Majesty had a very charming voice and that the Prince spoke excellent English considering he was German—and the lengthy prayers offered by the Archbishop of Canterbury, the organs and massed choirs once more exploded into Mr Martin Tupper's 'Exhibition Hymn.'

Scarcely anyone present failed to be moved by the spectacle. Tamsin noticed how even the Lord Chancellor was near to tears. Temporarily, all her senses were overcome by the atmosphere and she felt too small to contain her emotions. It was while the music soared around her that for the first time her eyes roamed from the dais. She glanced upwards to the gallery on the far side of the transept to discover that one pair of field glasses, unlike all the others, was trained not on the royal party and dignitaries but on herself.

Then the glasses were lowered.

Their owner smiled and bowed slightly.

Hot colour invaded Tamsin's cheeks. Even from this distance she could not fail to know the stranger from the conservatory. Fate, it would appear, intended them to meet inside glass buildings.

His smile deepened and she saw how his teeth gleamed. Memory conjured up the scent of Russia leather and macassar oil and the sensation of strong arms imprisoning her. Momentarily, she felt quite faint and began to fan herself with the souvenir programme. And, although she turned away her head, it was not quite quick enough for her aunt demanded:

'Do you know that person?'

'No,' replied her niece truthfully. 'I believe he mistakes me for somebody else.'

Fortunately, Aunt Scott was too engrossed in watching the Duke of Wellington chat with Mr Paxton to pay much attention to the gentleman opposite or notice Tamsin's discomposure, but she would most likely have attributed this to the heat and crush of people. All the same, she did not refrain from offering her usual monitory advice: 'Pray do not look towards him again, Thomasina, or he will think you are encouraging his attentions. Remember, Sir Everard, and doubtless this Mr St John, would disapprove of you being greeted by a strange gentleman, however accidentally, even at a gathering graced by royalty.'

Tamsin endeavoured not to look, but she was apprehensive lest he make some move in their direction, and so was compelled to peep over the top of the programme while pretending to study it with the closest concentration.

She was relieved rather than disappointed when, after the departure of the royal party, her aunt sighed: 'I think we should visit the Exhibition another day, Thomasina. It will prove far too fatiguing to attempt to see it properly after so much excitement. Besides, these new boots are pinching. I shall have a few harsh words to say to that bootmaker recommended by Mrs Edgecombe. Let us go home.'

Although she had intended to examine as many of the one hundred thousand exhibits as possible on this first day, Tamsin did not try to persuade her aunt to stay on. How mortifying it would be if *he* managed to waylay them and insist on claiming before Aunt Scott how they had already met at the Exhibition Ball.

Once, as they were making their way to the Edge-combe carriage, Tamsin thought she glimpsed him among the surging crowds, but could not be sure. And, on the homeward journey, she found herself anxiously glancing out of the small rear window just to ensure that no bearded, impudent-eyed gentleman was following their progress. What a nightmare come to life it would prove to be should he suddenly turn up on the Edge-combe doorstep. . . .

CHAPTER
THREE

It was certainly quiet in the house without Leonie and her mamma.

For Mrs Edgecombe had decided to accompany her daughter on the railway journey into Gloucestershire, having frankly confided to Mrs Scott: 'While I regret not being here to receive Mr St John, and must leave you and Tamsin until tomorrow, I feel it my duty to inform Septimus in person of his niece's waywardness. Besides, I prefer not to trust one of the maids to act as Leonie's chaperone in case my daughter talks her into some folly.'

She did not need to explain to Mrs Scott that 'some folly' might well involve the proscribed Mr James.

It was a matter of regret for Tamsin that the Edgecombes would not be present during her first meeting with Sir Everard's cousin. She trusted their lightheartedness to temper any fraught interview. It seemed obvious that Mr St John had come to inspect her in order to report back to his relative, much as he might have been sent ahead to examine a likely horse or a town house, to prevent Sir Everard from wasting his time.

Now, it would be almost more important to please this cousin than the actual suitor to ensure a favourable reference.

'And what will he say of you?' she consulted the reflection in the dressing-mirror.

'A missish creature without spirit—if you follow your good aunt's counsel,' returned the image.

'A frivolous minx if you model yourself upon Leonie,' warned the image.

'If Everard recalls you at all it is as a miniature hoyden with quick flying fists,' the image remarked nastily. 'And he has probably warned this cousin of your disagreeable temper.'

Tamsin bit her lip as memories of their final encounter flooded back. Perhaps it had been tiresome for a school-boy of some fourteen summers to be pursued around his papa's estate by a four-year-old moppet in short skirts lisping he must be kind to her as one day they were to be man and wife. But, he could have tried to be kinder for then her heart had worshipped him as a mighty hero and would have melted at one smile.

Her fingers clenched around the hairbrush as she re-called the skirmish from which she had been disen-tangled by a shocked and scolding nursemaid, but not before her little fist had blackened one of Everard's scornful eyes and bloodied his aristocratic nose, for he had declared he would rather wed a South Sea savage than give her his name. Her heart had been wounded and the scar had hardened against its assailant. From that day onwards she had taught herself to hate Everard Fortune, whatever others recommended to be her duty.

'I can only be myself,' Tamsin concluded, and then half defiantly: 'Whatever that is and whether or no it pleases Everard.

'Of course, were I courageous, I could always refuse to marry him.' At the mere idea of such disobedience Tamsin felt quite breathless, as if her stays had suddenly been jerked too tight. That would serve Everard right. For then he could not inherit his papa's great wealth and estates, and since he had been profligate in spending what Lady Fortune settled on him, or so it sounded from reports of his wild behaviour, he would find not marrying her a great deal more inconvenient than marrying her.

It soothed Tamsin's rancour somewhat to contemplate, however briefly, the effects of her rebellion upon Everard.

But, then her brain demanded, what benefit would you derive, miss?

To spend the rest of her days as companion to Aunt Scott, listening to reproaches about how she had foolishly and undutifully flouted her papa's wishes and forfeited Fortune's purse and person was a fate little better than marrying Everard.

For Aunt Scott had never minced words as to what Tamsin's prospects must be in the event of her not becoming Lady Fortune.

'If he doesn't marry you, miss, just who will, I pray you tell me that? Your reputation will be tarnished if he cries off. No proper gentleman is going to choose a penniless young creature as wife. Don't imagine I can afford to furnish you with a fat dowry simply because you're my brother's child. In my widowed state it has been difficult enough bringing you up properly . . .'

No doubt, exhausted by a surfeit of wifely duty and advice, Uncle Scott had succumbed to mortality long before Tamsin had come to live with his relict. She could just remember him as a jolly red face attached to a gold watch chain and smelling pungently of brandy.

'There will be nothing else for you but to become a poor thing of a governess belonging neither below stairs nor in the drawing-room, the object of every unchivalrous fellow's baser attentions. Remember, *I* only took you in after Roger's foolish accident for the sake of your poor dear mamma. I saw it as my bounden duty to bring you up and ensure none of his wicked ways took root in you and that any trace of sweet Isobel would be nurtured.'

Aunt Scott had never disguised from her niece how much she had pitied Isobel Lucas for being married to her brother—who, in fact, had worshipped his pretty, delicate wife—or that she held him responsible for breaking his neck on the hunting field through sheer carelessness and thus leaving her with his daughter to rear.

It was evident to Tamsin that while any element of her papa had been soundly stifled in her, the orphaned Sir Everard had been allowed a free rein to indulge in all his own father's excesses. For Sir Oliver had died shortly after Mr Lucas. Not on the hunting field, but in mysterious and scandalous circumstances, so rumour had it. Something to do with a married lady's boudoir. Tamsin had never been allowed to hear that story and could only imagine the worst, while not being entirely sure what the worst could be—which made the circumstances even more shocking.

Still surveying her reflection, Tamsin thought how reassuring it would have been to have Leonie there to advise her on the most suitable outfit to win Mr St John's approbation. After much careful consideration, and even more trying on and discarding of gowns which, depending upon the measurements of their waists, required Minnie's strength to loosen or tighten the strings of her stays, Tamsin selected an afternoon gown of embroidered muslin with bell sleeves. The skirt, pushed full by many petticoats, was open to reveal a top petticoat flounced and trimmed with the same white lace as the slender undersleeves. No one could deny the soft blue-grey shade set off her colouring, and Tamsin judged the effect to be subtle, although Leonie had discarded this simple cobwebby gown after one wearing, declaring it insipid.

It required even longer to decide how to dress her hair. Eventually, she parted it in the centre, looped the tresses low over her ears and twisted them into a huge shining knot at the back of her head. The style became her small features, making her appear demure and fragile beneath the weight of so much hair.

Almost a creature of porcelain and crystal, Miss Thomasina Lucas now appeared to be the sort of young lady who required to be most carefully taken care of by a strong and gallant gentleman. It was an appeal, according to all the arbiters of etiquette and good taste, no proper gentleman could resist in a wife. However, she had no idea whether or not Mr St John was a *proper gentleman* in the true sense of those words. Despite title and ancient lineage, his cousin certainly was not!

Before going down to the drawing-room she spent ten more minutes at the mirror repeating: 'Prunes. Papa. Potatoes. Prisms. . .' an exercise recommended by Miss Edgecombe for prettily shaping the mouth.

The richly furnished drawing-room was swathed in afternoon shadows, for the heavy window drapes had been half drawn to prevent any importunate sunbeams from fading the Turkey rugs and heavy flocked wallpaper. Aunt Scott was sitting in front of a large glass dome which protected a marvellous decoration of wax flowers and fruit and stuffed exotic birds that was much envied by all Mrs Edgecombe's friends. She was somewhat red-faced and irritable, having consumed her usual post-prandial glass of port mixed with brandy but, owing to the visit of Mr St John, without the customary rest

which normally lasted until tea-time peckishness roused
her.

She screwed her shortsighted eyes against the gloom
to inspect Tamsin.

'I trust you have not crayoned your brows, miss,' she
said, having detected how Leonie darkened hers with
the judicious use of a lead pencil.

'No, ma'am.'

'And all that hair is yours?'

'Of course.' Tamsin was rather proud of her hair
which was too luxuriant to need artificial aids for the
most elaborate arrangements, unlike Leonie's which required the discreet addition of a set of false ringlets for
evening wear.

'You will do, I suppose.' Aunt Scott's grudging approval was quite a compliment. 'I trust this Mr St John
will not keep us waiting.' Clearly she was not prepared to
like the gentleman any more than she liked her cousin. 'I
presume you will not sit idle while we await him.'

No longer did she add 'Satan finds work for idle
hands', but Tamsin knew it was implied, having heard
the maxim so often as a small child. Then, she had spent
many minutes contemplating her hands in fascinated
terror, trying to guard them against being overtaken by
some diabolical machinations.

'I am going to make a drawing for Leonie's album as a
surprise for her when she returns. She has presented me
with a beautiful flower painting on rice paper for my
album so I want to do my best for hers.'

'Evidently, Mr James's instruction was not quite
wasted,' observed Mrs Scott sarcastically. However, she
could not fault her niece's task, for she considered the
keeping of and contributing to albums a harmless and
suitable past-time for all well-reared young females, and

water-colour painting a skill no proper lady should be without.

Tamsin seated herself at Mrs Edgecombe's davenport in the window recess where there was most light, and began to sketch a nosegay of cornflowers, poppies and lilies-of-the-valley which she would colour later. By concentrating on this design in her mind's eye she tried unsuccessfully to rid herself of anxieties about the forthcoming visitor.

Soon the sound of rhythmic snores announced that Aunt Scott was taking her nap, sitting bolt upright with a lace-edged handkerchief covering her face. The Berlin woolwork with which she had intended to occupy herself had slipped unheeded to the floor.

Tamsin could safely allow her attention to wander.

She picked up Mrs Edgecombe's new kaleidoscope, shook it, and admired the beautiful coloured patterns which formed and changed beneath her gaze. Nervously, she twisted at the fringe of an embroidered runner that bisected one of the innumerable small rosewood tables which made crossing the drawing-room in a wide skirt a somewhat hazardous manoeuvre, particularly as most of them were scattered with an assortment of shell boxes, ornamental china and glass knick-knacks.

She might have allowed her mind to recreate yesterday's dazzling spectacle did it not always bring her back to the stranger and the fear that he might yet seek her out. Even within the kaleidoscope's ever-changing brilliance his dark eyes might be found laughing at her. Now and then, she peeped through the lace-veiled panes, hoping for a preliminary view of Mr St John, but he arrived while her eyes were fixed elsewhere for she only heard the loud rap of the knocker against the front door.

Almost at once Minnie entered, coughed in the direction of Mrs Scott, and announced pertly: 'A Mr St John is here to see you, ma'am.'

Aunt Scott struggled to consciousness, straightened her cap, tucked away the kerchief and retrieved the Berlin woolwork, before reaching for the visiting card on Minnie's tray. She examined it through her lorgnette, and her expression grew the more forbidding. 'Ask him to step in here, Minnie, and bring Madeira and ratafia biscuits.'

Mrs Edgecombe's cook made excellent biscuits, but Tamsin was sure this would be the one occasion when she was unlikely to notice if they tasted of sawdust.

She was tidying the pencils back into their box so that her back was to the door as Minnie announced 'Mr St John'; hence she heard the voice before she saw its owner.

'Good afternoon, Mrs Scott.'

Tamsin turned sharply. Only rigorous self-control stopped her crying out. Fortunately, Mrs Scott was too busy scrutinising the visitor to pay attention to her niece's expression, but had she looked in Tamsin's direction she would have seen eyes wide with fright, and the mouth, unmindful of 'prunes' and 'prisms', slightly agape.

Mrs Scott decided the gentleman's dark blue broad-cloth coat with its velvet collar was highly presentable, and so offered Mr St John her hand. Graciously, he bowed over it.

'May I present my niece, Miss Thomasina Lucas.'

The pressure of his handshake was brief. To Tamsin's ears her own voice sounded as if it came from very faraway as she bade him: 'Good afternoon, sir.' She raised her eyes to discover his almost black ones gazing at her face. Only by a whisper of a glance did he betray the fact that he recognised her.

Impostor! screamed Tamsin's mind. He could not be David St John, cousin to Everard Fortune. Yet, if he was not, what was he doing in this house flourishing the appropriate visiting card?

'Your servant, Miss Lucas.' The pleasant drawl had too deeply imprinted itself on Tamsin's memory for her to cling to the desperate hope that this gentleman merely resembled the stranger in the conservatory.

She knew with certainty that here was the man who had held her so passionately in his arms the other evening. Now, he was smiling politely towards her aunt. Her worst nightmare had come to pass.

'Pray be seated, Mr St John.' Mrs Scott was quite unaware of the charged atmosphere. She assumed Tamsin's pallor was the result of foolish nervousness and when Minnie re-entered bearing a tray, said briskly: 'Do allow my niece to pour you a glass of Madeira, sir.'

Aunt Scott subscribed to the philosophy that nothing soothed the fidgets and nerves of young females better than industry.

'That will be most pleasant, ma'am,' the gentleman said distantly, managing to convey that while he was delighted to accept hospitality he had no great compulsion to take wine at every hour of the day; and thereby earned himself a good mark from Aunt Scott who had heard that Sir Everard was regarded as a great tippler.

With eyes cast down, Tamsin handed David St John a glass of the amber liquid. She glanced towards her aunt who nodded eagerly: 'And take a glass for yourself, Thomasina. You are grown rather pale.'

The gentleman cast solicitous eyes on the young lady. 'I trust you are feeling quite well, Miss Lucas?'

'Of course she is,' returned Mrs Scott. 'When these

silly girls visit London they are so anxious to see and do
everything they quite exhaust themselves.'

Hastily, Mr St John sipped his wine. Only Tamsin
noted how a grin pulled at the lips above the pointed
beard. He knows full well why I am pale, she thought
savagely.

'And how is your cousin?' Mrs Scott enquired with
well-bred indifference.

Over the rim of her untouched glass Tamsin studied
Mr St John. The elegant wrapped cravat of dark blue
watered silk was tied in a large bow. Above it the countenance was pensive, as if the gentleman was trying to
decide the answer to a particularly tricky question. Dear
Heaven, she reflected wildly, now he knows who I am he
will certainly report my impropriety to Sir Edward, and
no doubt explain how the fault lay in the lady's com-
pliance rather than the gentleman's effrontery. If she
had not been so certain Mr St John had mistaken her
identity because of that ball gown she would now have
believed the whole incident had been specially contrived
by Everard Fortune to ruin her reputation. How they
will laugh together over it; and the sweetness of the
ratafia biscuit could not counter her inner bitterness.
Quite inadvertantly, Mr St John had presented his
cousin with the perfect egress. How could anyone in
polite society expect him to marry a shameless creature
who allowed strange men to embrace her?

'He is quite well, ma'am,' Mr St John replied
languidly. 'He begs your own and Miss Lucas's pardon
for his tardiness, but there is some outstanding business
which requires his immediate attention.'

Mr St John did not know Mrs Scott as well as her niece
and so could not read how disbelief wrote itself large
across her features.

'And do you reside in England, sir?' the cultivated tones suggested polite disinterest rather than the avid curiosity Mrs Scott contained with difficulty. Before very long she intended to know all there was to know about this tall gentleman with the dark curling hair.

'No, ma'am. I have been travelling on the Continent with my cousin for a number of years, in fact since we both came down from Oxford, acting as a sort of general factotum; making arrangements and going ahead to secure comfortable accommodation and such like. I am indebted to Everard, who, most philanthropically, has encouraged my scientific studies.'

Tamsin recalled Leonie's account of Baden Baden.

If Everard was expected at the spa what could have been more natural than for Mr St John to be there in advance? Presumably, he had kept his relationship with the notorious Sir Everard concealed from Miss Edgecombe or she would have been bound to mention how she had met this cousin, even if she had not admitted they were on kissing terms. Perhaps he did not wish the connection to be widely advertised in case it affronted young ladies from respectable families; yet his unchivalrous behaviour suggested he was as much a rake as Everard.

Tamsin's eyes grew unusually chill.

Mr St John would find it harder to dally with Miss Edgecombe in England, chaperoned as she was by a keen-eyed mamma anxious to protect her daughter from a misalliance. However, Tamsin was sure Mrs Edgecombe would consider Sir Everard's cousin a vast improvement on the drawing master, and encourage her daughter's acquaintanceship with him since it could be quite properly fostered through their friendship with Sir Everard's fiancée.

For the first time that day Tamsin was unaccountably

relieved that Leonie was absent. She would have to meet
Mr St John eventually, Tamsin supposed, and then he
would solve the riddle of the ballgown. At that meeting
would Miss Edgecombe betray how well they must have
known each other, and would she find this admirer from
Baden Baden quite as attractive now Mr James was
nearby? In his turn, would Mr St John be pleased to be
reunited with Miss Edgecombe?

Tamsin glanced about the room. There were no
likenesses of Leonie displayed. She could not help
wondering if Mr St John knew whose house he was in,
but perhaps he had no notion of Leonie's full name. . . .

So immersed was Tamsin in her own speculations
about Miss Edgecombe and Mr St John that she scarcely
heard her aunt echo suspiciously: 'Scientific studies.'

Science in itself Mrs Scott viewed as dubious for it
threatened to upset her ordered world with its dis-
coveries, but anything encouraged by that hellrake,
Everard Fortune, she felt must be undesirable.

'Yes, ma'am. I am most interested in photography
and the development of the portable camera.'

Mrs Scott nodded her grave assent. Previously, she
had entertained serious doubts about the respectability
of daguerrotypes and all other means of securing exact
likenesses by these new-fangled processes until she
learned how the Queen and Prince Albert were ardent
admirers of photography and had allowed themselves
and their family to be photographed regularly. Still, it
quite astonished her that Everard Fortune should support his cousin in anything so socially acceptable.

'And does Miss Lucas look forward to my cousin's
return?' Mr St John leaned towards Tamsin and she
could smell the scented macassar oil that gave his locks
the burnish of a blackbird's wing.

Is he mocking me, she wondered, flushing under the urbane smile which denied any secret stood between them. Yet he had no way of knowing her antipathy for Sir Everard.

Before she could volunteer a suitable response, Aunt Scott spoke in her stead: 'Perhaps you are unaware, sir, but the couple have not set eyes on each other since childhood. I think it would be presumptuous of Thomasina to express any feelings about Sir Everard. However, I am sure she will offer him her duty as she has been taught.'

Mr St John gave Tamsin a quizzical sideways glance as if trying to read her real feelings. No doubt, she thought, so he may telegraph them to his cousin.

'May I be permitted to express the earnest opinion that Sir Everard will be delighted when he meets Miss Lucas.'

Mrs Scott swallowed down the last of the Madeira and came as near to banging down a glass as gentility permitted. 'Perhaps. We had heard he has expressed to a number of people encountered on his travels how he would rather not wed my niece but that his inheritance depends on so doing . . .'

To accord Mr St John his due he did look quite uncomfortable which Tamsin thought honest of him. A very faint colour stroked his high cheekbones and embarrassment clipped his speech: 'I confess he has admitted as much to me. This is not Miss Lucas's fault, for my cousin is over-hasty and has enjoyed so much freedom that the responsibility incurred by matrimony may seem a little irksome. However, once he sets eyes on your niece I vow his doubts will be cast aside and he will embrace duty with a glad heart.'

Mrs Scott smiled grimly. 'A pretty speech, sir. Doubt-

less, your cousin chose to send you ahead because of
your talent to play the diplomat.'

Mr St John's lips twitched in the beginnings of a smile
but, as if judging this response to be ill-chosen, con-
verted it to an expression of gravity. 'I promise you,
ma'am, Sir Everard will say much the same when he
meets Miss Lucas.'

I cannot very well sit here as if I have lost the power of
speech, Tamsin thought desperately, yet what can I say
that will not be twisted so it can be reported to Everard
to my disadvantage, or reveal to my aunt we have already met? By little admonitory shakes of her head Aunt
Scott tried to encourage her niece to join the conversation. She had taught Tamsin a still tongue was an asset
but felt the girl was overdoing silence.

Mr St John appeared ignorant of any strained
atmosphere. 'Does Miss Lucas hope to visit the Exhibition soon? I attended yesterday's opening—a most awe-
inspiring ceremony, I do assure you. How well Her
Majesty looked . . .'

'We were there too, were we not, Thomasina?' and
Mrs Scott conclusively proved to Tamsin the short-
sightedness she was always denying, for she did not
connect Mr St John with the gentleman with field
glasses.

'What a pity I did not know. I would gladly have
escorted you both as would have been Sir Everard's
wish.'

He looked towards Tamsin blandly, denying he had
ever studied her through a pair of field glasses.

In spite of all Aunt Scott's assiduous training Tamsin
was aware the little hoyden still dwelt within her. How
she longed to take Mr St John by his fine shoulders and
shake him soundly for his humbug duplicity.

She sensed his eyes were laughing as if he could read her mind.

Mrs Scott could have no idea of the silent interchange between the gentleman and her niece and filled the lull with a question.

'Do tell us how you are related to Sir Everard?'

'The St Johns are on Lady Fortune's side of the family.' He grimaced slightly and paused: 'I'm afraid we are the poor relatives.'

Tamsin looked for signs of poverty on Mr St John. True, he wore but little jewellery: a heavy gold signet ring and a plain watch chain across the pale grey expanse of waistcoat, but she thought his well-cut clothes spoke of an expensive tailor. Perhaps he wore Sir Everard's cast-offs much as she did Leonie's.

'Have you spent very long with Sir Everard?' Tamsin enquired curiously.

Mrs Scott looked pleased. Not only had Tamsin broken her awkward silence but broached a question to which she too wanted an answer.

Mr St John nodded. 'We are around the same age, Miss Lucas, and went to school together and then the university. Of course, I could never have afforded to travel so I was overwhelmed by Sir Everard's generosity when he offered me the position of travelling companion. A poor relation must shift the best he can.'

A poor relation, mused Aunt Scott with slight pity, is forced to do the bidding of his patron, however distasteful he might find it.

Would Mrs Edgecombe and Leonie consider Mr St John quite as desirable without money? wondered Tamsin, and found herself smiling.

'Are your parents still alive?' Mrs Scott was a regular terrier when it came to nosing out information.

'They died long ago, ma'am.'

'And where did they live?'

However, Mr St John appeared not to hear her question for suddenly he clapped a hand to his forehead and exclaimed: 'My dear ladies, I had almost forgot my duty in all this pleasant conversation. I am here on Sir Everard's behalf and bring Miss Lucas a letter from him, and this . . .'

He extended a cinnamon brown chamois pouch secured at its neck by a silken thong.

Tamsin looked towards her aunt who nodded. Unwillingly, since she knew what it must contain, Tamsin accepted and untied the pouch. Inside was a worn black leather box which sprang open when she depressed the catch. On a bed of deep blue satin lay a ring of diamonds and emeralds fashioned like two hearts and surmounted by a lovers' knot.

Spontaneously she exclaimed: 'Oh, how pretty it is!'

'He will be gratified you like it,' Mr St John said gently. 'I believe it belonged to his Mamma and was presented to her by Sir Oliver on their betrothal. Will you not try it on, Miss Lucas?'

The ring felt heavy in her palm, heavier than its actual weight because of what acceptance of it entailed. Tamsin looked at it gravely, aware of the beauty and costliness. The few tiny pieces of jewellery she had inherited from her mother, it must be confessed, had been too paltry for Mr Lucas to sell in order to settle his numerous and recurrent debts. It would have almost been too easy for her to slip the sparkling band on her finger and admire the effect. And, yet . . .

Resolutely, she shook her head, closed the box and replaced it in the pouch which she set carefully upon a table.

'No, Mr St John. I am aware the honour your cousin does me by presenting this ring, but until he arrives and wishes, of his own free will, to place it on my finger I think it must remain safely in its box.'

SHe did not choose to look to her aunt for confirmation. Mrs Scott bit her lips, half tempted to intervene, but at the same time aware her niece had spoken soundly, if only for a girlish romantic whim. It seemed unnatural even to that most pragmatic of ladies that a gentleman other than a suitor should offer a young lady a betrothal ring.

Mr St John's own expression was somewhat enigmatic, but Tamsin sensed her refusal had somehow disconcerted him. Oh well, he would report it to his cousin who would either snigger or be angered, depending on his mood.

'Then, open the letter, Thomasina, do, and tell me what he writes,' commanded Mrs Scott.

Tamsin smiled a little ironically. There could be no embarrassment in obeying this order. It was unlikely the letter contained secret words of love and certainly no remembrances of shared stolen moments.

Sir Everard's handwriting was bold and spiky and easy to read. It was clear he was accustomed to giving orders and having them obeyed.

'"My dear Miss Lucas,"' she read in a quiet voice, but somehow the autocracy of the writer still seemed to pervade her tone. '"I much regret the necessity which keeps me from your side. May I recommend to you my cousin, Mr David St John, and ask that you treat him as you might a brother or a cousin, and know that he acts in my stead and with my full authority. Call upon him for any service you may require.

"My solicitors have given me to understand that you

and Mrs Scott are presently residing in a friend's house in order to visit the Exhibition and await my arrival. It would be preferable for you and your aunt to remove yourselves directly to my town house, number 32 Connaught Square, not far from Hyde Park. It is unnecessary for you to be beholden to friends when a house which will be yours in time stands empty. I have sent instructions for my Stillwater butler and housekeeper to arrange to staff the London house with a full complement of servants. I trust you and your aunt will find their ministrations to your taste and you will be quite comfortable. Order what you will in the complete knowledge that it is with my permission. Your most obedient servant, Everard Fortune.'''

There was insufficient space at the bottom of the sheet of paper so the final sentence curled round and up the side.

'There is a post script: "I trust you will find the ring acceptable."''

During the reading of this letter Mr St John had trained his eyes on one of Mrs Edgecombe's bright glass paperweights, as if he knew Sir Everard's words by heart and had no wish to show curiosity about any responses they elicited.

Mrs Scott examined her niece's tranquil face and sighed. She could not really fault the wording of the letter but thought it would have been more appropriate had Sir Everard expressed some kind of sentimental longing to see the girl he was to make his wife.

'I shall be sorry to leave here,' Tamsin admitted softly, 'and will miss the company of dear Mrs Edgecombe, and Leonie, too, when she returns to London.'

'I wonder at the propriety of staying at Connaught Square,' Mrs Scott voiced her anxiety. Was it quite suitable for them to stay in an unmarried man's house even though he was absent?

'I am convinced my cousin would wish you to entertain your friends in his house, Miss Lucas, particularly as they have been so hospitable. After all, he intends that you treat it as your home,' Mr St John assured her. He turned to Mrs Scott: 'It is a very fine house, ma'am, and servants are already installed and eagerly await your arrival. I have been there today to ensure all is prepared. Surely, nothing could be more proper than for your niece to reside in her future husband's town house.'

Mrs Scott could not refrain from feeling rather elated at the realisation she would be virtually mistress of so prestigious an establishment until her niece actually married Sir Everard. She envisaged entertaining Mrs Edgecombe in a drawing-room much more luxurious than the one where they now sat.

'Will you be able to move tomorrow?' Mr St John asked, noting Mrs Scott's rather smug smile.

'So long as Mrs Edgecombe has returned,' she agreed, 'It would be impolite to remove ourselves from here without first telling her.'

'Then I shall have the pleasure of meeting the lady tomorrow and will of course beg pardon on Sir Everard's behalf for robbing her of two such delightful house guests. Naturally, I shall escort you to Connaught Square to ascertain there are no problems.'

The dark eyes smiled kindly at Mrs Scott who grew quite pink. She had no wish to like Mr St John, but at the same time had to admit he possessed very charming manners—in spite of everything. She doubted Sir Everard would have spoken so thoughtfully.

At that moment Minnie re-entered the drawing-room to address Mrs Scott. It occurred to Tamsin that the

maid would be highly relieved when her aunt moved lest
suspicious eyes pry out her secret and report it to Mrs
Edgecombe.

'Sorry to disturb you, ma'am, but there's a person
here.' She eyed Mr St John, measuring the suitability of
mentioning the reason for the 'person's' visit before him,
and finally hissed: 'It's about your boots, ma'am.'

Mrs Scott looked a trifle aggrieved but all the same
rose to her feet. 'You will excuse me, sir. I shall be no
more than a few moments with the *person*.' She noticed
how pale and apprehensive her niece had suddenly
grown. Really, there could be no impropriety in her
being alone for a short while with the gentleman Sir
Everard had recommended they treat as a relative—
who, in fact, would be a relative in the near future. Had
she provided the silly child with too sheltered an
existence?

'Offer Mr St John more wine, Thomasina, and why
not show him the charming picture you are contriving for
Miss Edgecombe's album . . .'

It could do no harm, she thought, for Mr St John to
report Thomasina's accomplishments to his cousin.

Solicitously, Mr St John opened the drawing-room
door and Mrs Scott retired, her petticoats rustling like
crisp autumn leaves.

Tamsin poured wine into Mr St John's glass and re-
treated to the desk, rather to put greater space between
them than to exhibit the incomplete drawing.

Mr St John swallowed the Madeira with considerably
more enjoyment than he had demonstrated before Mrs
Scott. With a faint smile he studied the young lady who
leaned against the edge of the davenport, her hands
tightly clasped, but he made no move in her direction.

'He has come about her boots,' she explained to fill

the silence that lay between them. 'They pinch.'

Mr St John's laughter was as she recalled it before she knew his name.

'Uncomfortable boots are nothing to laugh at, sir,' she reproved primly.

Unsuccessfully, Mr St John attempted to stifle his mirth. 'I am merely astonished the boots had the temerity to behave so improperly towards your aunt's feet.'

Although Tamsin had intended to keep her expression very severe while they were alone a gurgle of laughter managed to escape her lips.

Mr St John helped himself liberally to another glass of wine. 'I am delighted you are human after all, Miss Lucas. I had begun to suspect my cousin was about to engage himself to a wax doll, albeit a very pretty one, but utterly devoid of conversation and emotion.'

'How can you say such a thing when you do not know me?' she demanded hotly.

'No, that is true, and something which must be remedied by regular contact.' He smiled wickedly, 'I must confess my amazement on discovering the fair unknown languishing in the conservatory the other evening was none other than Miss Thomasina Lucas, Sir Everard Fortune's bride-to-be. Fate plays ludicrous tricks on us human beings . . .'

'I beg, sir, you will not recall any of that evening,' and she was furious at the blush which suffused her cheeks and refused to be controlled.

'Why not?' he sipped the wine. 'It is something I wish to remember.'

'While I have every desire to erase it from my memory.'

'Because it was so unpleasant?'

Tamsin chewed at an index-finger nail, something

Aunt Scott would have condemned as unladylike. She did not dare tell him of the tumult of feelings his embraces had released within her. 'It would displease Sir Everard mightily,' she said at last.

'If you do not mention it to him I certainly shall not.'

'You vow that?'

'Of course. Anyway, as it was a genuine mistake, does it really signify?'

Tamsin was quite shocked at his casual approach to something she took so seriously; but, of course, if he were a rake like Sir Everard then the matter of an illicit kiss was of very little account. No doubt, Leonie Edgecombe was one of many conquests whose names he did not remember if he had in fact ever bothered to find them out. 'I understand your cousin seeks not to marry me. Do you not consider last evening's *mistake* would present him with the ideal excuse for jilting me?'

'That would depend on how much he valued your reputation,' returned Mr St John soberly. 'It appears you wish to marry him exceedingly.'

Tamsin began to twist her fingers in an agony of indecision. She scarcely dared confide to him her true feelings about Sir Everard. Tremulously, she said: 'I do not know.'

'I suppose his title, and the wealth which will be his when you two marry, are attractive inducements to a young lady, no matter what she really feels about the gentleman,' Mr St John jeered.

'No! No!' Tamsin's voice rose emphatically. 'You make me out a base creature when all I am attempting to do is my duty—a duty imposed upon me by my late papa. I do not really care for title and riches,' she paused and admitted: 'I have never known such things. But, my aunt insists that if Sir Everard finds a pretext to jilt me while it will not exactly enhance his reputation it will destroy mine completely. No one will ever want to marry me. At eighteen my life will be quite ruined.'

Her eyes darkened tragically.

A gentle smile replaced his sneer.

'We cannot allow that to happen, Miss Lucas.' He stepped towards her, and, before she could shrink from him, said: 'Here is my hand to seal the promise of silence.'

Once again, she shook his proffered hand, but this time to find the firm clasp as warm and lingering as his embrace. Then, quite unexpectedly, he raised the little hand to his lips.

Tamsin snatched away her hand as if the kiss had scorched her flesh. She looked up to see whether he mocked her and found his expression quite sincere. Indeed, there was no hint of the jocularity she noticed on his face following their encounter in the conservatory.

She swallowed quickly. 'I had best show you the drawing or my aunt will wonder what we have been discussing.'

Mr St John examined the delicate sketch, and listened carefully as she explained the design and the eventual colouring. Now and then, Tamsin stole a glance at his face to make sure he was really attending and was gratified and surprised to find his interest was not feigned. As they leaned over the sketching pad she could not but be aware of his proximity, and the bell sleeve's gauzey material seemed intent on caressing the dark blue masculine broadcloth cuff.

'I am sure Miss Edgecombe will be delighted when she sees this,' he remarked.

Tamsin pondered if she should acquaint him with the fact that this Miss Edgecombe, whom he appeared not to

know, was the original owner of the rose ballgown and
the young lady he had evidently met in Baden Baden. It
seemed slightly devious of her to withold such facts. And
yet, she comforted herself, it might do Leonie's reputation no good to reveal a secret until it need be known.

'What you attempt with pencil and watercolours, Miss
Lucas, I would endeavour to record with my camera.
Perhaps one day you will permit me to photograph your
likeness surrounded by flowers.'

'I . . . I don't know.' Tamsin wondered what her aunt
might think of this suggestion. 'For what purpose?'

Mr St John thought a little before answering. 'What
else but to send to Sir Everard so he may have a charming record of his future wife before they were formally
introduced to each other. He has often wondered what
you look like, since he can only remember you as a tiny
girl . . .'

And, although the answer sounded acceptable,
Tamsin found it gave her little satisfaction to think he
would make a picture of her merely to appease Sir
Everard's curiosity.

'What will you report to him of your meeting with
me?'

'That it was most agreeable,' came the prompt but
slightly ambiguous reply.

Tamsin reddened, and was tempted to retort: 'I am
talking of this afternoon, sir,' but feared Mr St John
might say: 'And so am I, my dear lady, so am I,' for then
she would look exceedingly foolish.

'Will I like Sir Everard?' she asked a trifle wistfully.

'How can I say?' Mr St John's response seemed
somewhat guarded. 'Some folk find him a good enough
fellow I suppose. Others deplore his unorthodox behaviour . . .'

She sensed he might have told her more, but perhaps he felt she would find the whole truth unappealing.

'And will you recommend me to him as the ideal wife?' she demanded slyly, putting her head to a side and balancing her chin on one forefinger. He saw that she was teasing him a little and was both surprised and delighted by this unexpected boldness.

'I would have to know the lady longer before making such an important judgment,' he returned, without smiling and looking long into her large grey eyes until she felt slightly dizzy and feared she must lose her balance and fall towards him.

There was no chance for Tamsin to put further questions for Mrs Scott re-entered the room, a somewhat triumphant smile on her face, having soundly trounced the bootmaker and received an abject apology and the promise of a new pair of kid boots.

Shortly afterwards Mr St John took his leave and promised to return the following afternoon to accompany them to Connaught Square.

Long after his departure, Tamsin sat in a low chair with the ring on her lap and the letter in her hand. Mrs Scott said nothing but watched her niece almost indulgently, assuming, not unnaturally, she thought of Sir Everard, without having any notion that however often Tamsin re-read his letter her thoughts dwelt not on the writer but the bearer. . . .

CHAPTER
FOUR

HAD Mrs Scott ever permitted herself the indulgence of wild dreams then the luxury afforded by the Connaught Square house would have fulfilled the wildest of them. She doubted if even the Queen received a greater deference from her servants than was shown to Tamsin and herself by the Fortune retainers. Almost all her anxiety as to whether or not it was quite correct that they reside in Sir Everard's town house was allayed by being cocooned among such undisguised riches.

True, Aunt Scott had not been sure of the propriety of some of the paintings and statues amassed by Sir Oliver. They were very large and magnificent, but the flimsiness of the subjects' attire was difficult to ignore. However, when Tamsin pointed out how most of these objets d'art were quite old and had been purchased abroad her aunt seemed to feel a degree of respectability was lent them by age and foreignness.

Tamsin would have been a very unnatural girl had she not been impressed and delighted by the splendour of Sir Everard's London home, but she could not help feeling she was caught in a gilded web spun by an invisible spider. Enmeshed in these trammels of wealth would she ever dare choose a different life if it were ever offered . . . a life that might not be endowed with sumptuousness? Now that her aunt had seen what marriage to Everard must invest in her niece she would have no sympathy with any girlish qualms at the prospect of marrying him and would exercise her utmost vigilence to ensure nothing hindered the wedding.

Indeed, thought Tamsin on the first night in her silk-hung bedroom, the world would consider me mad to want anything other than can be had by becoming Lady Fortune. She could well imagine Everard's chagrin at knowing this house, and goodness knows what other possessions, would only be his if he married silly little Thomasina Lucas or found a satisfactory justification for not doing so . . .

Of course, no time was lost in inviting Mrs Edgecombe to inspect all the glories of Sir Everard's establishment, and that lady was lavish in her praises.

'What a lucky, lucky girl you are,' she told Tamsin repeatedly, and sighed: 'Ah . . . if only my Leonie had shown the good sense to attract a suitor of such quality.'

Tamsin forebore to remark that her own good sense had absolutely nothing to do with Sir Everard Fortune becoming her suitor: if she possessed any it seemed to dictate quite another course of action.

'Still, my dear, it is all a little odd. I wonder if I should want things quite this way for *my* daughter.' Mrs Edgecombe paused to sip tea from a handpainted porcelain cup and help herself to a minute sandwich from the ornate silver basket which handle was decorated with the Fortune escutcheon.

'*His* absence rather recalls the story of Psyche, don't you think, my dears?' She giggled happily.

Tamsin glanced across at her aunt who had definite prejudices against ancient mythology, since she considered the behaviour of the gods, goddesses and various other mythological characters fell well below her own standards of moral rectitude.

Before Mrs Scott could intervene with the remark that 'Perhaps the story was not fit for a young girl's ears,' Mrs Edgecombe continued, blithely unaware: 'You know,

the nymph who married Cupid on the understanding she
would never try to see her husband. He transported her
to a marvellous palace—as fine as this no doubt—where
she could have anything her heart desired. Only at night
did Cupid visit her . . .'

Here Aunt Scott's lips pursed warningly.

'. . . but always left well before dawn. When Psyche's
sisters visited the palace they were consumed with
jealousy and hinted that perhaps her husband had a
monstrous appearance which was why he chose to remain invisible. Curiosity and no doubt fear prompted
poor Psyche to light a lamp to see Cupid while he slept.
She was enraptured by his beauty, but her disobedience
was discovered when a drop of hot oil fell upon her
husband and woke him. He fled. Psyche wandered in
search of him but she had incurred the hatred of Venus
who tried to prevent the lovers meeting.' Mrs Edgecombe tasted a sliver of rich fuit cake and sighed through
the crumbs. 'Ah, but in the end true love conquered:
Psyche was united with Cupid and endowed with im-
mortality.'

Tamsin thought it a charming story, although hardly
applicable to her own situation. She did not know what
appearance Everard now possessed: his debauches
might have made him quite hideous. Anyhow, she could
scarcely imagine herself becoming enraptured at sight of
him or wandering in pursuit if he fled!

Aunt Scott had no time for such romantic flummery
and commented scornfully: 'It is only a story, ma'am. I
fear a girl's head may be turned by these fantasies. This
can lead her along all sorts of undesirable paths, which is
why I have never encouraged Thomasina to read such
tales.'

By which she intended to imply that had not Leonie

enjoyed her fill of fiction and tinsel she might not now be
in disgrace at her Uncle Septimus's rectory.

Since Mr St John had not only escorted Tamsin and
Mrs Scott to 32 Connaught Square, but also visited them
daily to ensure all their wants were being provided, Mrs
Edgecombe could not fail to meet him, and after the first
introduction had pronounced him a 'perfect love'.

Tamsin noticed how he treated her rather differently
from her aunt, whose every word he appeared to regard
with the same gravity he might extend to Holy Writ.
While it could not be said the gentleman actually flirted
with Mrs Edgecombe, he certainly seemed to bring a
sparkle to her faded blue eyes and a coquettish giggle to
her lips. She had been a pretty girl, and, although
widowed with a grown-up daughter and a plump
matronly figure, still possessed a trace of that youthful
charm. It was rather delightful to have a gentleman smile
at her with those dark, worldly eyes and listen intently to
every word she uttered without the conviction that he
was merely pretending interest and wished to hurry
away from her company.

From the manner he adopted towards ladies Tamsin
deduced Mr St John was well versed in feminine
characters and so knew how to suit his approach to an
individual lady. Possibly he behaved towards her exactly
as he would to others of a similar temperament and
experience. But, of course, as she kept reminding herself sharply, such skills would be a rake's stock-in-trade.

Naturally, each time Mrs Edgecombe met him she
mentioned her absent daughter and always appealed to
Tamsin to corroborate her accounts of Leonie's beauty,
docility and maidenly charms. Most politely did David
St John listen to these maternal eulogies and Tamsin's
more cautious support, and expressed his hope of meet-

.ing Miss Leonie in the near future.

It tickled an impish corner of her sense of humour that he really had no idea he had already met Miss Leonie or that he trifled lightheartedly with the mamma of the young lady with whom he had flirted somewhat more seriously in Baden Baden.

Tamsin was quite baffled at her own relief that Mrs Edgecombe did not immediately recall Leonie. Apparently, her suspicions of the art master's charms outweighed her pleasure in those of Sir Everard's cousin.

It was not long before Mrs Scott saw it as her duty—a slightly malicious one, it might be admitted—to inform the fond mamma that however pleasant Mr St John might seem he was dreadfully poor and compelled to live off of Sir Everard's bounty.

Had Tamsin not been quite so overwhelmed by the giddy sensation each encounter with Mr St John somehow produced—and angered at this foolish reaction— she might have found Mrs Edgecombe's dilemma slightly amusing: while strongly approving the gentleman's appearance and family connections maternal wisdom could not allow her to overlook his impecuniosity.

Since their formal meeting Tamsin and David St John had been given no opportunity to converse alone for even one moment, and he always treated her with the rather aloof politeness that no one could fault but which she found curiously unsatisfying. Yet what else could she expect from him now their identities were revealed? From what he communicated to Mrs Scott Tamsin inferred Mr St John sent daily bulletins to his cousin about how niece and aunt fared at Connaught Saure. It appeared that Sir Everard replied as there were always fresh commands for the servants regarding the comfort of his guests.

Now that Mr St John had contacted them Sir Everard was somehow stirred into considering the well-being of his future wife, but Tamsin could not help believing she owed this to the promptings of the cousin rather than the genuine concern of the unwilling suitor.

Of course, it was most enjoyable to take full advantage of all that the Fortune residence offered. It was particularly pleasant to know the comfortable carriage was always available, and Mrs Scott and her niece had ridden in it several times to the Exhibition. Inwardly, Tamsin remained rather disappointed with these visits, for her aunt was only prepared to stay a short while, and then her interest was mostly directed towards items of wearing apparel, particularly a wonderful corset that somehow opened instantly in case of some sudden disorder. Even the chance of recognising a famous face did not compensate Mrs Scott for the inconvenience of having to mix with crowds and Tamsin feared she would never get an opportunity to see all the exhibits before the Exhibition eventually closed.

As the Connaught Square food and wine was even finer than that provided by Mrs Edgecombe, Aunt Scott could always be relied upon to require a lengthy nap after each luncheon. While thus engaged she assumed her niece was occupied in some equally laudable pursuit. There were more than enough duties to keep a young girl busy during those afternoon hours before Mrs Edgecombe or Mr St John might be expected to pay them a call.

Dutifully then, Tamsin always commenced the afternoon by sewing. Now that Sir Everard's return could not be relegated to some uncertain future date Aunt Scott had decreed the embroidering of some monograms on the trousseau linen must begin—a Sisyphean task—for no sooner had Tamsin finished neatly stitching one item than there was yet another to complete. Aunt Scott had counselled the design of the initials 'T' and 'E' entwined within a heart; and while Tamsin sewed she could admire this pretty conceit yet smile sardonically at its total inappropriateness.

After an hour of this exacting needlework she longed for some air, and would don bonnet and short cape to slip out into the quiet street. Since Tamsin was almost always within sight of the house there seemed little impropriety in her taking a stroll about the handsome square; and naturally she arrived home well before Mrs Scott stirred. She was particularly grateful to the taciturn and efficient servants who never thought to mention her brief outings; but doubtless they saw nothing untoward in Miss Lucas's walks.

Tamsin had been indulging in these harmless excursions for about a week before meeting anyone she knew. Then, she noticed standing at the north-east corner of the square the slight figure of a young man dressed in pale grey she felt sure she recognised. Seeing Tamsin emerge from the imposing front door by herself the gentleman began to walk in her direction. Suddenly, he hesitated as if reconsidering. When eventually she drew level with him he raised his hat and her recognition was confirmed for the gentleman was Mr Elliot James.

'Good . . . good afternoon, Miss Lucas,' he stuttered apologetically, and his cheeks flushed a deeper crimson than hers. Tamsin felt quite sorry for him: obviously he was embarrassed and somewhat in awe of her, which was a pleasant experience for a young lady who had never imagined any man could be nervous of her.

'Good afternoon, Mr James. Do you visit pupils in Connaught Square?'

He blushed even more painfully and shook his head. 'No. I . . . I learned of your change of address a few days ago,' he faltered.

'Minnie?' she enquired gently.

He nodded and swallowed. 'I took the liberty, Miss Lucas, of standing on that corner, hoping to catch a glimpse of you so that if you were alone I might perhaps ask . . .'

He hesitated, as if wondering how best to phrase his question.

'You wish to ask me about Miss Edgecombe?' she prompted, feeling rather protective towards him.

He nodded sadly. 'You are her friend, and I am sure she confides to you the secrets of her heart, and that therefore I may trust you.'

Tamsin smiled reassuringly and he continued:

'Do you know if she intends returning soon?' his tone was desperate. 'I have not received a single note from her since she informed me of her exile. I had even begun to wonder if she has changed her mind about us . . .' he stumbled to a miserable halt.

'I daresay her letters are closely supervised by her uncle,' Tamsin said consolingly. 'For she writes only to her Mamma enclosing messages for me which say little beyond that she is well and hopes I am enjoying London. Reading between these lines I suspect she is bored and unhappy and that time hangs heavily on her hands. But, as for when she will return, sir, I have no idea. I do not think Mrs Edgecombe has quite decided. I am certain, however, Leonie regrets being away as much as you regret her absence . . . and for the same reason.'

'Do you really think so?' For a moment his woebegone expression was animated by hope.

'Of course. I had rather thought you might travel to . . .' It was Tamsin's turn to falter.

Was it improper, she wondered, to remind him that Leonie had assumed he would follow her into Gloucestershire?

But, Mr James was eager to explain: 'I cannot depart for a few days, not until my pupils leave town. If I did I would lose a good part of my living, for on their return they would seek another drawing master—one they considered to be more reliable.'

Tamsin nodded. It was evident that Mr James loved Leonie but had to temper his yearning to see her with the necessity of earning his living.

'Do you think she will understand?' His anxious brown eyes pleaded for a kindly response.

'Of course. Perhaps if you were to seek her Mamma's permission to see her, Mrs Edgecombe might grow less opposed to the idea of your friendship with Leonie. I imagine she is distressed because you have both behaved in such a deceitful manner.'

Mr James chewed his lip with furious concentration. 'Believe me, Miss Lucas, I have no wish to be underhand in this matter. Were I to beg Mrs Edgecombe to grant me permission to pay court to her daughter I know full well what her answer would be. My intentions towards Miss Edgecome are the most honourable any gentleman may offer a lady, but an unconnected, penniless artist is not considered a suitable candidate for her hand. So we have little other choice but to resort to clandestine meetings. We had not seen each other for an age before that ball. Can you understand how much we longed to be together?'

'I think I can,' Tamsin said slowly, aware her own life had not provided her with enough experience for a more positive reply. It was impossible to imagine casting all caution and propriety to the four winds to secure a secret rendezvous with Everard Fortune, and in fact she could almost chuckle to herself at so preposterous an idea.

She did hope Mr James would never know just how little Leonie had apparently considered him in Baden Baden, for in her own mind Tamsin was convinced the drawing master's devotion was genuine, without any underlying mercenary motives. At least, Uncle Septimus's forbidding presence would prevent Leonie from flirting with another to wile away the time. Tamsin was quite alarmed by the cynicism of her own thoughts.

Idly, she glanced across the square to notice another gentleman entering it. How could she fail to recognise Mr St John's rather jaunty step or the way he swung the malacca cane as he walked, having watched him through the drawing-room window as he crossed the square after his daily visits? Sometimes he would turn and look at the house, as if to discover if someone did observe him from the windows, but Tamsin always managed to conceal herself behind the heavy velvet curtains—not only to prevent him learning of her curiosity, but also to conform to her aunt's dictates that it was improper for young ladies to gaze out of windows at departing guests. She had never been able to explain satisfactorily to herself just why she was so interested in Mr St John: was it only his relationship with Sir Everard, or did it have something to do with their first meeting? Perhaps it was unwise to seek the correct answer to that question.

Mr James had not noticed how her attention had been distracted or that her eyes suddenly blinked with surprise. For, even as Mr St John raised a hand, presumably to doff his fine hat, he seemed to glance at her com-

panion and change his mind. Whereupon, instead of
crossing the road towards them, he deliberately turned
on his heel and was soon rounding the corner out of
sight.

What on earth is he about, Tamsin asked herself? But
Mr James was speaking and she had to bring her
thoughts back to their conversation.

'Miss Lucas, will you find a way to convey some message to her why I must stay in London a little longer? I
know it is impertinent of me to involve you, but I believe
you are our friend in this . . .'

'I shall do my best, Mr James, but it will be difficult.'
As she promised Tamsin knew that should her role be
discovered Mrs Edgecombe would scarcely thank her
for abetting the couple.

Mr James seized her hand, pumped it heartily, then
remembered himself and released it as if it were a live
coal. 'I beg your pardon, Miss Lucas,' he gasped, red-
dening yet again. 'But we shall be eternally grateful for
your help. I shall endeavour to be in the square each
afternoon around this o'clock in case you have any news
for me.'

He gave one more nervous smile before hurrying
away.

Tamsin nodded distantly, for her mind was no longer
on poor Mr James's problems. She had the horrid pre-
sentiment that perhaps Mr St John had returned to his
Baker Street lodging to pen a letter to his cousin with the
damning news that Miss Lucas had been discovered
trysting with a young man a few steps away from Sir
Everard's own house.

But surely, she thought wildly, he must realise were I
to do something so indiscreet I would select a less public
meeting place.

As she continued to walk about the square she brooded upon Mr St John's puzzling retreat. The stroll that usually refreshed now made her feel tired and nervous. Hearing the tattoo of quick footsteps she turned to see Sir Everard's cousin rushing after her and stopped to allow him to catch up.

'I did not want to intrude upon your conversation,' he said promptly.

'It would not have signified. I would have introduced you to Mr James, who met Sir Everard in Paris.' She deemed it sensible to make him party to the drawing master's tribulations.

'So you understand,' concluded Tamsin, 'I must try to help them even if only by penning a letter which will be understood by Leonie and not by her uncle in case he insists on perusing all her letters.'

Mr St John smiled and quoted: '"The course of true love never did run smooth." Is this drawing master so unsuitable for Miss Edgecombe?'

Tamsin thought it comic they discussed a lady he thought he did not know, and she half wondered if her motive for confiding Mr James's and Miss Edgecombe's romantic secret might have something to do with Mr St John's eventual reunion with the girl he had met in Baden Baden, for then he would know she was promised to another.

'He is poor,' she explained.

Mr St John made a bitter face.

'And you consider that a serious shortcoming?'

'Of course not,' Tamsin retorted. 'But her mamma does . . . and most of polite society, too, as you must have noticed.'

'Then I presume I shall never marry,' he said pensively, 'Since I have no sufficient financial inducements to win myself a wife.'

Tamsin would not look up at him but concentrated instead on twisting the fringed ends of her bonnet strings with slightly agitated fingers. 'I am certain you will find a lady willing to marry you for yourself if that be your desire.'. How she wished her voice would not tremble and her cheeks had not contracted Mr James's distressing blush.

'Do you think so?' But the dark eyes seemed to be putting some other unworded question.

Yet, such as he would scarcely choose to marry, Tamsin realised, for by choosing one lady the freedom to pursue as many as his fancy prompted would be seriously curtailed.

They strolled together in thoughtful silence until, remembering that etiquette demanded some uncontroversial topic of conversation flow between a gentleman and a lady, Tamsin enquired: 'Have you paid many visits to the Exhibition, Mr St John?'

'Not as many as I should like, Miss Lucas,' came the polite response.

'Nor I,' she admitted and sighed. 'I fear Aunt's suspicion of crowds and the dubious skill of the bootmaker will prevent me from ever seeing as many of the contributions as I should wish.'

Mr St John took her arm to guide her across the street. Tamsin willed him not to read the thoughts which rose unbidden to her mind: how different was this light impersonal pressure of the hand beneath her elbow from that other almost savage grasp of another time.

'Perhaps you would allow me to escort you to the Exhibition, Miss Lucas, and thereby save your aunt from constricting boots and tiresome crowds.'

Momentarily, her eyes kindled with pleasure. Then,

adamantly she shook her head: 'That, sir, is quite
impossible.'

'Because you do not choose to have my company?'

'No,' she returned with a conviction which made him
grin. 'But Aunt Scott would consider my acceptance of
your invitation as vastly improper.'

'I can't think why,' he said mildly. 'I am sure Sir
Everard would not view it in such a scandalous light.
What could be more natural than his cousin escorting
you in his absence? With your permission, I shall say as
much to your aunt this very afternoon.'

'Will you really?' Tamsin gasped, much impressed.

He began to laugh merrily. 'It is not quite as dangerous as placing my head in a lion's mouth. Besides, I have
begun to detect that Mrs Scott is most anxious not to
offend Sir Everard, so that if I suggest to her that this
excursion would be according to his wishes I doubt we
will have very much opposition.'

'But, suppose she insists on chaperoning us?'

Mr St John cast an amused look at her doleful expression. 'Ah, so you do long to be alone with me—even
amidst all those crowds.'

'No.' Tamsin blushed crimson. 'You misunderstand
me purposely. If she insists on coming then we shall see
one or two exhibits—' she doubted Aunt Scott would
gaze upon the corset in Mr St John's company, 'before
going home to rest her poor feet.'

He grinned. 'I shall take care of everything.'

And Tamsin could not help believing his assurance.
She stopped suddenly: 'May I ask you a favour, Mr St
John?'

'Anything, my dear Miss Lucas,' he teased, laying a
hand upon his heart so she could not help laughing at his
drollery.

'My aunt does not know that I take an afternoon walk in the Square. It is such a trivial thing, but I fear . . .'

'You prefer that I do not mention how we met this afternoon—and certainly not that you were sighted in the company of the lovelorn Mr James. Very well. My lips will be sealed on this matter as on others which *you* desire me not to recall. . . .'

Tamsin wished very much that her bonnet had a veil to cover her confusion, for it must have been very clear to Mr St John that she was remembering everything which ought to be forgotten.

'There is a great deal you are unable to do, poor Miss Lucas, in your unescorted state,' he remarked kindly. 'However, when my cousin claims you much will be remedied.'

Tamsin shrugged. She could not imagine that Sir Everard's presence would permit her any greater freedom than Aunt Scott's. It would merely mean a different range of activities as selected by him.

'Oh, I doubt Sir Everard will wish to ride on an omnibus.' She gave a small self-deprecatory laugh.

'And you do?'

She nodded almost shamefacedly.

'What a strange girl you are, Miss Lucas.'

'I am sorry,' she said humbly.

'You need not be.' He smiled, as if he recalled something pleasant. 'While other gentlemen might be able to spread jewels before your dainty feet,' he said lightly, 'I, at least, may be able to supply your current heart's desire. Now, go indoors.' He drew out a plain gold hunter and consulted it. 'I shall call upon you in about twenty minutes when I am sure I can persuade Mrs Scott to my way of thinking.'

As she entered the house and mounted the staircase to

her bedroom Tamsin was conscious of her heart beating almost too painfully, as if she had been running—or sustained some shock—and might require the aid of a smelling bottle. She had noticed this sensation often occurred in Mr St John's company: somehow the most ordinary words he uttered had the power to scare her and yet at the same time she felt compelled to seek the protection of the one who exercised this very curious influence. . . .

'You must be able to charm birds from trees,' she remarked to Mr St John the following day as he escorted her through the Exhibition's northern entrance. 'I have never known Aunt Scott accede to anything out of the ordinary with so small a struggle.'

Mr St John laughed at his companion's serious face. 'It was not very difficult to convince her once I explained it was Everard's wish that you see as much of the Exhibition as possible. Now, may I compliment you on the charm of your appearance, Miss Lucas. I must be the luckiest man in this glass palace to have the company of so amiable and pretty a lady.'

She was never sure whether his compliments were quite devoid of gentle mockery, but all the same it was pleasant to hear such praise, particularly as she had spent some hours in preparing herself for this most unexpected of outings.

From the gowns bequeathed to her by Leonie she had chosen one of blue gauze, the narrowness of its waist emphasised by pleats extending from each shoulder to a point at the waist. Over it, she had donned a waistcoat of deep blue velvet exactly matching the ribbons on her small cabriole bonnet and the bands at her wrists and throat which protected the uncovered flesh against the sun's rays.

'You look,' he added appreciatively, 'like an English summer morning beside the river. How envious must all those fellows be of my good luck!'

''Neither they nor you are here to admire me,' Tamsin said haughtily. She had decided the best way to avoid those feelings Mr St John somehow provoked in her was to treat him as severely as her aunt would do.

Unfortunately, Mr St John did not seem to react to her manner with the similar seriousness he offered Mrs Scott. Instead, he laughed as if he did not believe in Miss Lucas's severity and thought her attempts at it highly diverting.

'Very well,' he said, taking her arm and piloting her through the throng in the eastern nave, 'let us first concentrate on what the foreign exhibitors have to show us . . .'

For the next few hours Tamsin enjoyed herself more than she had ever done in her entire life. Not only was she permitted to gaze at the exhibits for as long as she chose without an acid voice bemoaning the state of its feet or the uselessness of the object, but was also, through Mr St John's thoughtful offices, given the best vantage point at the front of any gathering of people examining an exhibit, which was invaluable for a young woman possessed of diminutive stature and flat-heeled white kid slippers.

By choosing to visit the Exhibition in the early afternoon they had missed the crowds who came each morning to see the Queen who was methodically examining all the exhibits. Fortunately, too, they had selected a pound day, so the crowds were nowhere as great as those when the entrance fee was only one shilling, and since Tamsin possessed a season ticket she did not feel she was a financial burden to Mr St John.

'But, how well-behaved and well-dressed are all those who do come here on shilling days,' he remarked, for it appeared he often chose those days for his visits. 'I do enjoy the good-humoured jostle, and ordinary people are so interested in everything, unlike some of the rich and worldly who feel they have seen all life has to offer and are unimpressed by novelty.'

'I am afraid my aunt would never come here at such a time,' Tamsin told him smiling. 'Apart from the fact that she believes it is the haunt of rogues and vagabonds she does not approve of what she terms the Industrial Classes mingling on equal terms with their superiors, or seeing so many innovations, or even travelling on the railway. She thinks they will become discontented and that will lead to revolution.'

'But do you not agree it will rather encourage folk to broaden their horizons and so improve their lives?'

'Oh yes,' Tasmin said enthusiastically. 'But, aunt— like so many of her generation—is fearful of change in the social order. She believes much trouble is saved when people know their places, be they high or low.'

Never before had she indulged in so serious a conversation, for Aunt Scott had warned her that gentlemen do not like ladies to be 'blue stockings', yet here was one clearly content to talk seriously on any subject with her, and in turn listen to her opinions without treating her like a foolish schoolgirl.

And how fluently he explained the most complicated piece of machinery, so that it did not remain a mystery to a young lady who had never previously even heard of it. Tamsin was entirely grateful to him, and Mr St John seemed delighted to have a companion to share his interests with a similar zeal.

Some of the exhibits from the United States par-

ticularly intrigued them. There was a marvellous new
material called india rubber which could be manufactured into a score of useful objects, and a machine for
making ice, which Mr St John told Tamsin did so
through a process involving sulphuric acid.

She was greatly relieved Aunt Scott was not present
when they reached what was evidently the most popular
of the American attractions: a statue entitled 'The
Greek Slave', depicting a young woman with her hands
bound by chains and her clothes in a heap at her feet.
With some tact and not one facetious remark did Mr St
John lead her from this spectacle back to the French
section where she cooled her blushes admiring the Au-
busson carpets and Sevres china, and had to agree with
him that although the Queen of Spain's jewels were
magnificent they were eclipsed by the British ones, especially the Koh-i-noor diamond, shown in a large golden
bird-cage, and recently presented to Her Majesty by the
East India Company.

Tamsin was thrilled to discover one part of the Exhibition hall transformed into a real Tunisian shop where a
Tunisian gentleman bargained with members of the
public over the prices of calabashes and carpets, ignor-
ing the rule that nothing other than guide books, religi-
ous tracts, copies of the 'Exhibition Hymn' and refresh-
ments were to be sold.

'Exactly like Tunisia,' exlaimed Mr St John delightedly.

'Did you go there with your cousin?'

For a moment, he seemed unaccountably taken aback
and then, as if remembering something, he nodded
vigorously.

Tasmin's face grew troubled. She had almost forgotten she shared his company only because of whom she

must marry. She doubted very much that Sir Everard
would have paid her similar careful attention had he
even been bothered to escort her to the Exhibition.

'You are fatigued,' said Mr St John with concern. 'Let
us go up to the first-class refreshment rooms where we
may sit down and quench our thirst. I am afraid we can
obtain nothing more fortifying than Messrs Schweppes
bottled lemonade, but I imagine that is more of a hard-
ship for me than for you.'

Eating and drinking in a public place was something
Aunt Scott had never countenanced and Tamsin found
the novel experience so entertaining it scarcely mattered
what was offered. However, while Mr St John ate a fresh
Bath bun with evident appetite, she partook of an
orange jelly—something she had never before tasted
and which she pronounced 'Delicious!'

Mr St John appeared to enjoy watching Tamsin eat
this confection almost as much as she relished eating
it.

'It is most refreshing,' he remarked smiling thoughtfully, 'to be with a young lady who derives delight from
the smallest thing and has not adopted a world-weary
attitude to all life has to offer.

'I am certain it will be the Fortune cook's pleasure to
provide her little ladyship with as much jelly as she
desires,' he added cheerfully, and was somewhat puzzled that for a second the light seemed to fade from his
companion's sparkling eyes. In order to rekindle it he
added: 'If you are quite rested I am going to take you
along to my favourite section, but on the way we must
stop to admire Messrs de la Rue's incredible envelope-
making machine . . .'

'I shall never write or receive another letter without
recalling this.' Tamsin was quite breathless with admira-

tion after they had watched some forty-five envelopes being manufactured in precisely one minute!

Not surprisingly, Mr St John's favourite section was Philosophical Instruments. Here were to be found various cameras, meteorological, horological and surgical instruments, and Tamsin considered herself fortunate to be accompanied by a gentleman who knew so much about each extraordinary-looking piece of apparatus.

After he had explained to her the wonders of the stereo-scope – an instrument through which two pictures of a single object appeared as one, causing it to stand out in a solid form as in nature, Mr St John confided: 'I am trying to devise a portable camera so small it can fit in the top of an ordinary walking stick, or some other unlikely object, where it would not be easily detected.'

Tamsin was mystified. 'Whatever for?'

'Then photographs may be taken of persons without drawing attention to the photographer, which will be particularly useful when gathering information secretly, as in detective work.'

She could not refrain from laughing up at his earnest face.

'What a devious mind you possess, Mr St John. I am sure it is not at all proper trying to catch people unawares.'

'Ah, but it can be rather pleasant,' came the immediate riposte, and she was forced to hide her mouth behind gloved fingers, understanding too well that he was speaking of a matter which had nothing to do with photography.

All the same, she could not help musing how worthwhile it would be for a woman to encourage him in his work. How pleasant it must be to share one's life with someone who had such enthusiasm and inventiveness and wished to make a way for himself in the world. A man like Everard Fortune, whose interests were merely ways of filling in time for an over-indulged rich man's son, only required a wife to secure his inheritance and give him an heir, not to be a true helpmeet to share his pleasures and woes. . . .

Realising the implication behind her thoughts made Tamsin grow pale and cold. She must not compare Mr St John with Sir Everard as if she had a choice of suitors. She must forbid herself such perilous speculation, for it hinted she could be developing some feeling for the gentleman standing beside her quietly explaining how the camera obscura worked. She darted a sideways glance at him. Clearly, he would not entertain any affection for one destined to be his cousin's wife anymore than she could be allowed to think seriously of any man save Everard. Besides, the kind of lady Mr St John might eventually select as a life's partner—once his carefree bachelor days seemed less attractive—would be a much more dashing and worldly creature than Thomasina Kate Lucas.

Mr St John was unaware of Tamsin's change of mood, for his own attention had been distracted from the camera by the approach of a group of top-hatted gentlemen. From the expression on their faces Tamsin was certain they knew him, yet she must have been mistaken for Mr St John seized her arm and said urgently: 'Come, Miss Lucas, it is getting late. We must leave now.'

He hurried her away towards the southern exit without even pausing to allow her to admire the collapsible piano intended for use aboard gentlemen's yachts. Once, Tasmin looked over her shoulder. The gentlemen were standing staring after them and she thought they seemed rather perplexed.

'Do you know those gentlemen?' she asked somewhat breathlessly as they stepped into the cooler air of the Park.

'Which gentlemen?'

For all his bland ignorance Tamsin could not help sensing he had chosen to cut some persons he must have known since they recognised him.

If so, this would be the second occasion on which he had deliberately avoided a confrontation, for she was convinced he could have had no good reason for hurrying away when he saw her conversing with Mr James, except that he had no wish to be introduced to the young drawing-master, since he had sought her company directly she was alone.

There was a good deal more to Mr St John than initially met the eye, and, as Tamsin reminded herself sternly, some of his secrets might be unsavoury. After all, to be Sir Everard's boon companion over so many years would entail sharing some of his depraved appetites. If he treated ladies similarly to how she suspected he had behaved with Miss Edgecombe no doubt there were furious papas, or brothers, or even husbands seeking revenge.

Once away from the Exhibition's precincts Mr St John's urgency was forgotten, and he seemed disposed to saunter through the Park until he stopped to smile down at her and say: 'Now, Miss Lucas, if you promise not to breathe a word of this to your worthy aunt I shall be delighted to fulfil one of your ambitions.'

'What can you mean, sir?'

'Nothing shocking, I assure you.' He grinned at the suspicion in her tone. Then, a trifle ruefully: 'Nor costly I fear, since I am not very well-heeled. How would you like it if I were to escort you on a twopenny omnibus ride along Oxford Street?'

She had been feeling somewhat tired from all the walking they had done within the Exhibition's galleries, but the prospect of realising so delightful an aspiration immediately dispelled fatigue. And, by her smile, Mr St John could have no doubt she accepted his invitation with the greatest of pleasure.

They did not have to wait very long for the arrival of an omnibus. As he helped her step aboard Mr St John noted how she glanced longingly upwards and promptly guided her up the steep steps on to the open top of the vehicle where they had to sit very close together on the uncomfortable knifeboard benches.

Up here, a soft breeze tossed the ribbons of the women's bonnets, fanned flushed cheeks, and impudently plucked at hems to reveal ruffled petticoats and clocked silken hose. Tamsin was most relieved by the decency board which bore an advertisement for mustard and concealed her ankles from the world.

Obviously, other couples chose to sit on top to escape prying eyes, and Tamsin quite blushed for some of the young ladies who were indiscreet enough to allow their escorts to place an arm about their waist. Quite definitely, Aunt Scott would have been much horrified that her prim little niece should be exposed to such company.

But, how exhilarating it was to sit high up there and look down on the busy shops, with their signs swinging in the wind, the milling crowds and the assorted carriages which made even an omnibus's progress along Oxford Street a very dilatory business.

Now and then, their 'bus would jolt to a halt, as the driver was forced to rein in the horses because some hansom cab had, without due warning, swerved across

his path. On top of the 'bus the young ladies screamed
with terror and were embraced and comforted by young
gentlemen delighted to be of such service, while below
drivers hurled imprecations and untangled whips and
generally provided a diverting side-show for onlookers.

Once, Tamsin was thrown against her companion,
who placed a firm, steadying arm about her shoulders, so
that for an instant she nestled in his warm embrace.
Then, she was horribly conscious that those breathless
nervous feelings had returned. They reminded her viv-
idly of childhood when she had been made giddy by
swinging too high or whirling around too quickly. The
sensations were disturbing, yet not at all unpleasant.

They did not talk much but seemed to sit in a mutually
content silence, occasionally smiling at each other as if
they were very old friends, and Tamsin wished the
journey might take forever.

They returned by omnibus and when they reached the
head of Oxford Street, in order to help her from the 'bus
Mr St John caught her by the waist and swung her down
on to the pavement as if she weighed no more than a
single flower, laughing all the while she protested her
bonnet would be knocked askew by his reckless behaviour. And, long afterwards, the heat from his hands
seemed to grip her more tightly than the closest
stays. . . .

On the steps outside number 32, Tamsin paused and
said shyly: 'How shall I ever thank you sufficiently for
giving me such a wonderful afternoon, Mr St John? I
shall never forget your kindness and generosity.'

He bowed slightly but ignored the proffered hand
from which she had withdrawn its glove. His smile was
polite, even cool, the dark eyes had lost their warmth
and friendliness to brood on some remote matter. She

sensed a great distance had suddenly separated them.

'It is my pleasure to ensure Sir Everard's future wife enjoys her stay in London,' and the formal tone belonged to a stranger.

Tamsin's eyes became two storm clouds. No doubt, he now had a rendezvous with another lady, and had merely been marking time until the appointed hour. While she had imagined David St John to be enjoying their informal excusion just as much as she he was merely doing his duty for his patron. He may even have been bored by her naive company, but as one used to bending to the whims of ladies in order to toy with their affections he had been well able to mask it.

Probably each detail of the afternoon would be recounted to Sir Everard. The omnibus rides and his flirtatious attentions might even have been little traps set to prove her unsuitability for the role of the next Lady Fortune.

CHAPTER
FIVE

'WHAT sheer arrogance!' Anger painted Aunt Scott's complexion a deeper blue than ever portwine managed. 'His High and Mightiness does not request us. He commands.'

She had just perused the letter Tamsin had silently handed her, which had been delivered through Graveny and Hampden, addressed to 'Miss Thomasina Lucas'.

It seemed Sir Everard had decided the gaiety of London might prove too taxing for Miss Lucas, and therefore he had made arrangements that she and Mrs Scott should travel on the morrow to the tranquillity of Stillwater, where he hoped shortly to join them since he had little interest in being in town while it was so crowded with visitors to the Exhibition. Besides, he felt it less likely Miss Lucas would meet with any undesirable elements in a quiet country atmosphere. Accordingly, he had already sent instruction as to which rooms were to be prepared for them, and that the house in Connaught Street be closed.

'He is fortunate to have such efficient servants,' Tamsin remarked absently, for her mind was lamenting there might be no further opportunity to sample all the novelties of the Exhibition. Everard still possessed the same power to destroy her simple joys as when she was a tiny girl, and that certainly boded no good for their future mutual reconciliation. 'Mr St John tells me the housekeeper and butler at Stillwater have been there since Sir Oliver's day and so knew Everard as a child.

They, together with the solicitors, engage all his household staff for whichever establishment he chooses to open.'

'And I expect it costs him a pretty penny too,' observed Mrs Scott tartly. 'The sooner he has a wife to superintend his household affairs, the sooner will he begin to save money.'

'The sooner he has a wife,' Tamsin added, 'the sooner will his father's wealth be entirely his and he will have no need to practise economy.'

'And I was just beginning to settle down in this house,' complained her aunt. 'Now we shall have to start afresh in new surroundings where there is no one we know. It will be exceedingly tiresome.'

'Perhaps Mrs Edgecombe might be persuaded to join Leonie at the rectory,' said Tamsin, brightening at the thought. 'Then we shall have company nearby. As I dimly recall, Stillwater is very beautiful. The gardens are magnificent, and there is even a little maze beside the river.' These details had adhered to her memory since Stillwater was the scene of her final encounter with Everard.

'And, if he intends keeping that beautiful place he needs you as his wife,' muttered Mrs Scott with a sort of grim triumph. That the overweening Sir Everard could not get matters all his own way was some balm to her injured feelings, and the notion of entertaining Mrs Edgecombe in surroundings even more splendid than 32 Connaught Square also revived her spirits.

She did not doubt Leonie's mamma would deem it as essential to choose this time to stay with her brother, for then she and her daughter were bound to meet Sir Everard from the outset of his reunion with Thomasina. Soon Mrs Edgecombe would be able to boast she was

one of Sir Everard's and Lady Fortune's oldest friends—
a worthwhile social cachet for any mother with a marriageable daughter!

Only when she reached the penultimate paragraph did
Mrs Scott again explode: 'We are even told how we
should travel. By train! Because *he* has shares in the
Great Western Railway line which crosses Fortune
lands. Two seats are reserved for us in the posting carriage.' Grudgingly, she admitted: 'That is more comfortable than first class, which is something in its favour . . .
I suppose.' She rapped the letter with an admonishing
finger. 'The journey from Paddington to Swindon takes
two hours. Unnaturally fast. Man was never meant to
travel at such speed. The Stillwater carriage will meet us
at Swindon and convey us a further fifteen miles to
Stillwater itself. I fear that by the time we arrive we shall
be half dead from exhaustion.'

Tamsin forebore to remark that such a swift journey
would in fact save them much fatigue, for she knew Aunt
Scott would not have accepted her logic since she appeared to believe that speed could only be attained with
the active co-operation of the passengers.

Like her idol, the Duke of Wellington, Mrs Scott had
always deplored the inception of the railway, and for
similar reasons: it encouraged the lower orders to travel
around when they might have been industriously occupied at home. However, she was ignorant of just how
much her niece thrilled to this modern form of travel, for
Tamsin would hardly have dared voice her enthusiasm
since it ran counter to her aunt's opinion. If there was
any consolation to be had from leaving London in order
to meet Everard, it would be the actual journey.

'Do you suppose Mr St John will be our escort to
Stillwater?' Tamsin spoke her own thoughts aloud.

In the week following their excursion to the Crystal Palace he had punctiliously visited Connaught Square each afternoon to engage in polite and uncontroversial conversation with her aunt, never mentioning any details of their outing which might contravene Mrs Scott's code of conduct. While he always showed her every solicitude, Tamsin could detect nothing of the warmth she had felt existed during some of their moments together at the Exhibition. She sensed that somehow Mr St John had become withdrawn, as if he had lost any personal interest and was merely carrying out some obligation. Which, of course, was how it should be; although, as she was bound to admit to herself, it was not quite what she would have preferred. One fact she had noticed: he had suddenly grown singularly averse to escorting them anywhere, even for a brief drive in the park.

Mrs Scott raised her lorgnette to consult the letter again, and sniffed ferociously: 'It says nothing of Mr St John here. I doubt Sir Everard advised his cousin of this new plan. Otherwise, I am convinced Mr St John would have alerted us. Now, there is a gentleman with a modicum of delicacy and some sense of how matters should be arranged for ladies . . .'

Rare praise indeed from Aunt Scott, who viewed the entire male species under the age of seventy with mistrust.

'But, I suppose,' she added gloomily, 'it is his position in life which encourages a certain humility, whereas Sir Everard's whole existence is dedicated towards autocracy.' She gave the writing paper an angry prod with her lorgnette, 'Not to say total tyranny.'

Had their visit to the Exhibition anything to do with deciding Everard that she should leave London? Tamsin

found herself speculating, and if so, did Mr St John
accompany her there and on the omnibus rides with the
sole intention of provoking such a prohibiting response
from his cousin? While she did not wish to harbour base
suspicions of his motives, she could not overlook that his
loyalty lay with his cousin, and he might be playing some
deeper game which was directed to securing her down-
fall and Everard's consequent release. He might even
have become so bored with dancing attendance upon
Miss Lucas and her aunt that he had contrived a way to
whisk them from London and leave him free to enjoy all
the pleasures town had to offer until Everard required
his company.

'Perhaps Everard will be awaiting us at Stillwater,'
Tamsin remarked dismally.

'Well, if he is,' came her aunt's grim rejoinder, 'I
intend to tell him a thing or two about ordering folk
around without giving a thought to their comfort.'

How sadly comic, reflected Tamsin. Poor aunt is torn
in two opposing directions by Everard's character. On
the one hand she cannot fail to be impressed by his
lineage and the trappings of potential wealth. On the
other, she cannot fail to be aggrieved by his reputation
and manner. Since she could not enjoy the former without the latter Mrs Scott was faced with a dilemma she
was unable to resolve merely by doing her duty.

'It will be pleasant to see Leonie once more,' said
Tamsin, and deduced from her aunt's pursed mouth this
pleasure was not shared.

However, Mrs Scott was not to realise her niece
welcomed seeing Miss Edgecombe for a particular
reason. Only then would she be able to explain in detail
how Mr James intended to come to Gloucestershire as
soon as possible.

She had managed to pen Leonie a brief note which she had artfully asked Mrs Edgecombe to enclose in one of her own letters to her daughter. Even Uncle Septimus would not suspect a missive sent by his sister. The good lady was far too certain of Tamsin's uprightness even to read the sheet of paper handed her, although she did notice in passing it contained a small riddle.

Since both girls were particularly fond of enigmas, puzzles, spelling bees and charades this was hardly surprising; their albums were filled with examples gleaned from friends and every new acquaintance. It was every young lady's ambition to invent, or find, a riddle previously unknown to her peers.

Without mentioning Mr St John, Tamsin had written Leonie a brief account of some of the more memorable exhibits at the Crystal Palace and also described her room at Connaught Square. She had ended by remarking that: 'London is so crowded that certain people would dearly love to escape from it to visit the delights of the country, but responsibilities prevent them from doing this as quickly as their inclination would dictate.'

She relied upon Leonie's not inconsiderable cunning to link this mundane general statement with the riddle which followed:

'My position is number twelve in your letters;
Unlike mine which is a Roman 'V';
Warm 'e says if 'e is a cockney gent.'

It was not the best conundrum she had ever invented because there had been no time to polish it, but she was sure one glance from Leonie's sharp eyes would unravel it: 'L'; 'E'; 'ot' . . . or Elliott!

Because there were so many preparations to complete for their journey Aunt Scott took but a brief nap, allowing Tamsin only a few minutes grace to slip into the

square. A timorous Mr James awaited her on the corner
as he had done around the same hour most afternoons.

Breathlessly, she conveyed to him the news she would
soon see Leonie.

He smiled and stammered: 'And . . . I . . . I . . . too
shall be leaving for Gloucestershire in a day or so. Ah
how happy I shall be to look on the dear girl.'

'Then we may meet there, Mr James.'

'I do not know, Miss Lucas,' he said dubiously, 'for I
must keep my presence in that district a secret or else
they will send her somewhere else. If you do recognise
me perhaps it would be wiser for you not to acknowledge
me.'

Tamsin could not help admiring his steadfastness. She
thought it must be rather wonderful to inspire such
affection. Leonie, she was sure, would use her arrival in
the neighbourhood to cover up any secret meetings that
could be arranged with Mr James, for Mrs Edgecombe
was bound to countenance her daughter paying as many
calls as she chose to Stillwater, particularly as she knew
Mrs Scott would be in attendance, prescribing filial modesty and obedience in all things. Who Miss Edgecombe
might encounter on the way to or from the future Lady
Fortune would probably not occur to her mamma.

As she sped back to the house Tamsin grew aware of
how painful it must be to be separated from the one
person you most deeply cared for. It would be like losing
part of your self, and her face was still solemn with these
imaginings when Mr St John paid his customary call.

Evidently, he had not been apprised of their imminent
departure, for he greeted the news with bland assur-
ances of both ignorance and disappointment which
Tamsin was forced to believe, or else count him as good
an actor as Mr Charles Kean.

'So you will not be accompanying us,' Mrs Scott said with regret. She had become quite accustomed to Mr St John's presence and had rather hoped for his protection on their hazardous journey. If a gentleman could seize the bridle of a runaway horse she supposed he might do the same with one of those infernal steam engines which, in her opinion, were far less biddable than a pack of wild horses.

'No, ma'am, but if you will permit it I shall be here first thing in the morning to escort you to Paddington and see you safely aboard the train for Swindon.'

'Do you think your cousin will be at Stillwater when we arrive there?' Tamsin asked reluctantly.

'I am sure he would wish to be once he knows Miss Lucas is anxious for his company.' Mr St John's reply was gallant but scarcely helpful. And, he could not know why she gave him a sad little smile and shook her head, for she had just realised this might be the last afternoon visit Mr St John would pay them.

Before they left number 32 next morning a note was delivered by hand from Mrs Edgecombe, informing them of her surprise at their news. She considered it only sensible to rejoin Leonie at her brother's rectory and accordingly would be leaving the following day so that they would all be united very soon.

'What did I tell you?' remarked Mrs Scott with profound self-satisfaction.

Tamsin was grateful for the thick veil on the grey travelling bonnet, which concealed her grin. It struck her as somewhat ironic that Mrs Edgecombe and Mr James might well travel by the same train.

True to his word, Mr St John, most elegant in a dark brown morning coat and top hat, escorted them to Paddington Station. The Fortune carriage conveyed them to the platform so they had but a few steps to walk to their train.

Clouds of swirling steam obliterated the sky, and the hubbub and bustle from passengers and the rattle of luggage wagons might be heard before they loomed through the billowing smoke. The ladies were thankful for veils and enveloping cloaks which may have been over-heating but did protect them from drifting deposits of soot and grit.

Mrs Scott regarded the snorting 'Iron Duke' engine with considerable alarm, as if it had recently escaped from a menagerie and might devour the onlookers, but she had to admit that against the fresh brown and cream paintwork its brasses gleamed like burnished gold. She was somewhat mollified, too, at sight of the posting carriage, for it possessed all the small comforts of a modest parlour, and the few other passengers already seated in there were of the most genteel sort, while its clerestory roof provided plenty of light but excluded much grime and smoke.

'I suppose it might be worse,' she remarked, as if she had fully expected to find herself travelling in one of the third class carriages which were open not only to all the elements but also to soot and flying cinders.

'Believe me, ma'am, the Queen travels in a railway coach not dissimilar to this one,' Mr St John assured her, doing much to assuage any lingering doubts about propriety and safety.

From the Fortune equipage he retrieved a small wicker luncheon hamper which he stowed on the unoccupied seat opposite theirs. 'I have taken the liberty of providing you with a little sustenance for the journey, ladies, for tedium can prick the appetite as much as exercise.' He lowered his voice confidentially: 'In case you should feel faint or cold, ma'am, I have included a flask of some spiritous refreshment and two glasses.'

So well attuned was Mr St John to her aunt's foibles that Tamsin could not but suspect he had closely questioned Sir Everard's servants at Connaught Square about Mrs Scott's eating and drinking habits. If so, she wondered dismally, was he merely being thoughtful of their comfort or spying for Everard's information?

Mrs Scott had thrown back her veil so all could mark how her eyes glowed with appreciation. She held out her hand and shook Mr St John's most cordially. 'We are so grateful for all your consideration, dear sir, and shall inform Sir Everard as soon as we see him how kind his cousin has been to us, shall we not, Thomasina? Indeed, I doubt if he could have been more thoughtful.' This last was uttered without a trace of sarcasm, but her niece could not refrain from thinking had their companion been Sir Everard his treatment of them would probably have been far less kindly.

Tamsin could not speak at once for the nervous lump, which had first entered her throat when she recalled her meeting with Mr St John in the conservatory, had returned and threatened to bring with it foolish tears. She raised her veil and Mr St John's heavy dark brows drew together questioningly at sight of large grey eyes so revealingly bright.

'I, too, must thank you, sir, for all your kindnesses to us,' her voice trembled. 'We shall never forget you, and hope it will not be long before you visit your cousin's Gloucestershire estates.'

Mrs Scott heaved an inward sigh: the silly child still seemed as nervous of Mr St John as when he paid them that first call. How would she ever go about in society as Sir Everard's wife if she did not master her trepidations?

Quickly, Tamsin readjusted her veil lest her eyes tell tales best left unrelated. Mr St John gave the small hand a perfunctory shake and looked over its owner's head rather than down into her face. Miserably, she deduced: he does not care to prolong the business of leavetaking. Indeed, his: 'Farewell, dear ladies, a pleasant journey,' was uttered so abruptly it seemed certain urgent matters occupied his mind and he was anxious to depart to attend to them. Tamsin could not overlook the fact that he had said nothing about hoping to see them again soon. . . .

She and Mrs Scott had only just settled back in their upright cushioned seats when a piercing whistle announced the train's immediate departure. There were warning shouts, running footsteps, slamming doors—and Mr St John hurriedly descended from the posting carriage. Then, with a violent lurch, the train began to steam away from the platform.

Both Tamsin and Mrs Scott waved their handkerchiefs at the tall figure who was soon swallowed from their sight by distance and clouds of steam.

Perhaps he did not even wait to watch our train leave, thought Tamsin, but hurried away, the memory of Miss Lucas, now she was no longer his responsibility, fading as swiftly as the smoke from the departing train.

As the engine gathered speed she could almost believe it was doing Sir Everard's bidding by tearing her away from London—and all she held precious.

Held precious, echoed her thoughts. . . .

With a flash as bright and sudden as any celebratory firework against the backdrop of night, understanding of her own emotions exploded in the darkness of her mind to illumine the truth she had tried to ignore.

She knew without any doubt she had fallen in love.

With David St John.

Tamsin stole a quick frightened glance at her aunt who was contentedly sucking a peppermint lozenge against heartburn and gazing out at the marvel of the Hanwell viaduct as the train roared across it, oblivious of her niece's moment of self-revelation and that the girl wrestled silently with thoughts and emotions she was ill-equipped to command.

Tamsin clenched her fists and squeezed her eyes tight shut in an effort to deny the knowledge which caused her so much pain. All her reading of poetry and novels had not prepared her for this anguish. Why, oh why had it happened to her? She had never sought to complicate her life like Leonie by refusing to do her duty or opting for unwise but thrilling alternatives. Now the idea of marriage with Everard was even more repugnant than formerly. Her true affection must always remain unspoken and unrequited so that the rest of her life would be spent mourning what could not be.

And, as for the gentleman who lay at the heart of her problem, and was the problem of her heart, he would scarcely welcome her love or allow himself to fall in love with the future wife of the man on whom he depended for his own material wellbeing. No . . . not even if he found her nature and appearance pleasing, which was doubtful. A philanderer who could have his pick of fair creatures would scarcely see the unworldly Miss Lucas as the most alluring of them.

You foolish, foolish chit, Tamsin scolded herself in terms worthy of Aunt Scott. Because you have no experience of the world and have ever abhorred Everard you have allowed yourself to become enamoured by the first personable gentleman to pay you polite attention, even though he only did so out of duty, and all because of a forbidden kiss from one who wantonly bestows and receives such embraces.

As the other passengers began to delve into their own luncheon baskets Aunt Scott judged it proper to open theirs and prepared herself for whatever it contained by first taking a small glass of something fortifying. How right Mr St John had been: the railway journey certainly stimulated the appetite. It must be something to do with the speed.

'Do put up your veil, Thomasina my dear, so you may eat something. I must say this potted meat looks very tasty. There is sliced tongue. And beef. And a good wedge of Double Gloucester and white rolls and butter. Ah, and under this linen napkin, a handsome custard tart.' Mrs Scott delivered her inventory with pronounced fervour. 'Mr St John has done us proud. There is enough here to prevent us arriving at Stillwater in a state of ravening hunger. I should not like Sir Everard to think we were greedy.'

'A speck of dust must have entered my eye.' Tamsin's voice was subdued as she fought to control her tears. She threw back the veil, hoping her words would satisfy her aunt's curiosity as to why her eyes might appear red and watery.

Mrs Scott gave the pale tragic face a shrewd glance. She supposed the girl was grieving that her meeting with Everard could not be postponed much longer. In time she hoped Thomasina might find the material benefits sufficient compensation for having a husband she did not love. It was sad, but it was a fact of life other women often had to endure for the sake of duty.

Tamsin ate little, convinced each mouthful must choke her and bring about a storm of weeping. Through a haze of unshed tears she watched the lush green

countryside rush by. It was pretty and tranquil but did
nothing to soothe the pain. The journey she had thought
to enjoy had lost its savour. That a train travelled so
much faster than any horsedrawn carriage was scarcely a
reason for jubilation. Every churn of steam, every turn
in the track, drew her nearer to Stillwater, Everard
Fortune and marriage and further from London, David
St John and happiness.

To avoid any conversation with her aunt which might
include mention of Mr St John she pretended to
doze. . . .

She must have slept, for the next thing she was aware
of was her aunt gently shaking her shoulder.
'Thomasina, we are at Swindon. Straighten your bonnet. Come, let us descend and find Sir Everard's coachman so he may fetch our baggage.' She glanced at the fob
watch which had belonged to her husband and clicked
her tongue incredulously. 'We have reached here in such
a short time I feel it cannot be entirely civilized.'

The Stillwater coachman and footman had soft
Gloucestershire accents and greeted the ladies off the
London train as if they were minor royalty which Aunt
Scott much appreciated. It was quite a relief to be
piloted away from the steam, noise and bustle of the
platform and helped into a high, old-fashioned carriage
drawn by a pair of gleaming chestnuts.

'It is not as warm as it looks,' said the coachman
kindly, urging his passengers to wrap themselves in the
heavy wool travelling blankets. He added apologetically: 'I'm afraid the journey to Stillwater will take nigh
as long as did your train ride to Swindon, although we
have a much shorter distance to cover. But I warrant it'll
be quieter and free from smoke.'

He gestured to an ebonised, brass-inlaid box fitted to

the interior of the carriage. 'Perhaps you ladies will take a little refreshment.' He lifted the lid to reveal a travelling tantalus with four full decanters and plenty of square-based glasses slotted into the small doors.

Mrs Scott glanced at her niece's shadowed eyes and unnaturally pale cheeks. 'Come, Thomasina, you will take some portwine,' she said briskly, 'it is excellent for the blood. By your appearance I judge you are in need of strengthening. I believe all that speed has quite weakened you.'

Dutifully, Tamsin sipped the heavy sweet liquid and felt its warmth race along her veins, but somehow it failed to melt the chill in her heart or prise the sadness from her thoughts.

As they bowled along the narrow, leafy lanes and through small golden-stoned villages, scents of May blossom and cottage roses wafted into the carriage. Mrs Scott leaned back against the leather upholstery and expressed herself content. 'This is a much more pleasurable way of getting about. All that chaos, smoke and haste makes my nerves quite jagged so that I am continually feeling I've forgotten something important.'

Tamsin nodded her understanding, too listless to defend the merits of railway travel. She wondered if Everard awaited their arrival with the same lack of enthusiasm she entertained.

In the late afternoon they passed through handsome iron gates and past a neat lodge. A gardener doffed his cap and smiled welcomingly, clearly curious to glimpse Sir Everard's bride-to-be. Tamsin was suddenly aware that the servants were probably looking forward to having a married master in residence and that her arrival represented an important turning-point to all the Fortune retainers.

Stillwater was far more beautiful than ever she recalled, and Aunt Scott voiced her own satisfaction with the old-fashioned manor house built in traditional Cotswold stone which glowed a warm gold in the westering sun. Lawns, as smooth as the green baize on Mrs Edgecombe's card table, rolled down to the bank of a lazy, trout-filled river. Bright flower beds, as neat as embroidered gardens, dotted the grounds.

Much to her surprise there was nothing wild or untended about the place, for Mrs Scott had half suspected that Sir Everard's absence and eccentricity might have transformed it into a bat-infested ruin set amid a wilderness where she and Thomasina would be confined as virtual prisoners ministered to by crabbed, resentful servants. Having seen this second of the Fortune homes she decided that, whatever Sir Everard's disposition, Thomasina was a lucky girl and should forthwith cease moping!

Carefully handed down by the footman, Tamsin stepped onto the gravel court where she had last set a much tinier foot some fourteen years before. Would she recognise any trace of the boy, Everard, she just remembered, in the grown man, Sir Everard? Did his face even now peer from some upstairs window in order to gain a preview of the future Lady Fortune?

But these questions went unanswered, for they were ushered indoors by Merten, the butler, and Mrs Coles, the housekeeper, who bade them a cheerful but deferential welcome with one breath and with the next informed them that although Sir Everard was expected any day he had not so far arrived, and they still had no idea whether or not he had even landed in England.

However, they appeared to be thoroughly accustomed to their errant master's ways and looked for-

ward to his arrival at whatever hour of day or night. In
the meantime they and the rest of the household would
make it their pleasant duty to ensure his special guests
had all their wishes satisfied. . . .

It was two days before Tamsin and Mrs Scott felt
sufficiently recovered from the journey to pay a call on
the Edgecombes at Fairford. During that time Mrs
Scott's approval of Stillwater, and its management, had
magnified. If possible, they were being even better cared
for here than at Connaught Square, and Thomasina was
treated as mistress in all but name, although quite rightly
she deferred all important decisions as to choice of
menus to her much more experienced aunt.

That Mrs Scott had been so abruptly removed from
London, and by an infernal roaring iron contraption
too, was almost forgotten. The peaceful pleasures and
table of Stillwater provided ample compensations. How
much she looked forward to regaling Mrs Edgecombe
with an account of the possessions contained in the
Fortune manor house as well as its number of rooms,
the extent of its outbuildings, gardens, woodlands and
farms.

As the open landau carried them to Fairford she
leaned back as comfortably as her stays would permit
and surveyed her niece with disgruntlement. The wide-
brimmed straw bonnet and the apple-green voile gown,
both trimmed with rose ribbons, were most suitable for
an informal summer visit in the country, but they would
have been so much more becoming had only the
wretched girl looked less mournful. The child was lost in
thought and gazed apathetically across her aunt's shoulder in the direction from which they had come without
remarking on anything.

At least, some of that ghostly pallor had faded but why

wouldn't she cheer up and recognise her good fortune when it stared her in the face? It seemed to Mrs Scott that despite her rigorous training some of Leonie's romantic nonsense must have infiltrated her niece's skull, and she was longing for more from life than she should properly or dutifully expect. It was, thought Aunt Scott severely, most provoking of her!

The carriage trundled down into a dip where the pretty village of St Adwyn forded a stream. Outside the rustic inn, with its gently swinging signboard depicting a vivid rising sun, stood a post chaise, and Tamsin watched idly as an ostler helped the sole male passenger unload some bulky items of baggage.

The traveller was attired in a voluminous coat and a most ruffianly low-crowned large-brimmed hat which looked as if it had known better days. His boots were scuffed and dusty. This rough appearance together with a multiplicity of chattels suggest some kind of pedlar.

The 'pedlar' turned to say something to the ostler and Tamsin saw he was laughing so hugely that he had to clap one hand to his hat to prevent it tumbling off.

She started violently.

Mrs Scott did not remark on this agitation but noted only how her niece's cheeks had deepened to the shade of the ribbons on her bonnet and gown and that her eyes were wide and shining, but she quite sensibly attributed this rapid change to her own desire for the girl to be of good heart—once again proving the lamentable shortness of her own sight.

Tamsin almost doubted the reliability of her vision. Could her senses be playing tricks with her sanity? Surely, she recognised this roughly clad person. For he was none other than the gentleman she saw each night in her dreams since leaving London . . . the gentleman she was most diligently schooling herself to forget . . . and the gentleman she would never have credited as being the possessor of such unfashionable garments.

She was about to exclaim: 'Aunt! Aunt! Pray, tell the driver to stop!' when some inner caution seized her tongue. A welter of suspicion replaced any desire to speak out.

What on earth could the usually fashionable Mr David St John be doing outside an inn not many miles from Stillwater in the attire of a common packman? If he had intended to be so close to his cousin's estate only a few days after their own departure would it not have been more natural to give them prior intimation of his intentions? And, surely it would have been the most normal action in the world for him to come immediately to Stillwater—if not to stay beneath his cousin's roof, then certainly to pay his respects.

From his apparel and clandestine arrival Tamsin was compelled to conclude David St John had elected to come there for some nefarious purpose. And, she could not help discerning Sir Everard's hand in this mystery.

It might well be he had ordered his cousin to disguise himself and follow her secretly to put into practice some wily scheme to discredit her which would prove easier to execute on Sir Everard's own territory rather than in the larger world of London. Perhaps, indeed, that was why Sir Everard had commanded her immediate removal to Stillwater. Only such a conspiracy would explain David St John's unannounced presence and extraordinary appearance.

As the colour faded from her cheeks Tamsin resolved to banish absolutely from her heart any thought of trusting David St John, even if he did call upon them at Stillwater clad in his usual garments. Painfully, she realised there could be no pleasure in knowing of his proximity since his arrival in the neighbourhood rendered him an object of deep suspicion. . . .

CHAPTER
SIX

LEONIE had been right on one matter: her Uncle Septimus and Aunt Sophronia proved to have much in common with Mrs Scott, and it was not long before the three of them, and a slightly less enthusiastic Mrs Edgecombe, were engaged in deep debate in the gloomy drawing-room as to the iniquities of the younger generation and all those who flouted the advice of their wiser elders. The flow of conversation was greatly enlivened by elderflower wine which Leonie's aunt recommended as most health-promoting.

Consequently, Tamsin and Leonie were free to wander arm-in-arm in the rectory gardens and talk as if they had been separated for years rather than days, secure in the knowledge that their conversation could only be overheard by the bees murmuring among the roses.

Despite her protests of being bored to distraction and unhappy beyond belief, Miss Edgecombe looked very well and modish in a ruffled, deep blue silk gown. Manifestly, she had solved the riddle Tamsin had sent her, and now made her friend repeat every detail of the meetings with Mr James at least five times. At last, she preened herself like a most contented peacock, assured of his devotion by Tamsin's description of the misery in his eyes. It was most gratifying to be so deeply loved.

'Thank Heaven, my best-beloved Elliot will soon be here,' she murmured. 'It has been excessively dull. Of course, during Uncle's interminable sermons on Sundays I have been observed, and . . .' she giggled, 'much admired by the local young gentlemen. None of them is very fascinating, although Aunt Sophronia was most zealous in pointing out to me the worthier ones . . .'

Tamsin knew she should not be astonished that Miss Edgecombe could still seek fascination in any gentleman other than her 'best-beloved Elliot'.

Happy to have her friend's company once again Leonie squeezed Tamsin's arm. 'The only gentleman of interest hereabouts is of course *your* Sir Everard . . . that is, if only he were hereabouts. Dearest, do say when you expect him to arrive. It is most vexing of him to keep us all on tenterhooks.'

Tamsin shook her head absently.

Leonie took her by the shoulders and looked into her face. 'Dearest, you are so wan and thin. I trust you are not going into a decline like some maiden in a novel. But that is always caused by a broken heart, and yours is, I am sure, quite whole! Has Aunt Scott been horrid to you, or did you overtax yourself walking about the Exhibition? You are not still fretting about your betrothal, are you? Everard really cannot be as vile as he is painted.'

Tamsin tried to instil her smile with a gaiety she did not feel. 'I believe I am fatigued from travelling,' she said quietly. On no account would she confide to Leonie the problems Sir Everard's cousin was causing her, for that would entail revealing her very private feelings.

As if drawn to the subject by an invisible magnet, Leonie demanded inquisitively: 'And this cousin of Sir Everard's: Mr St . . . St James.' She laughed, 'how that name sticks in my mind. No. St John. Was he a boring old stick, or quite a dashing person?'

Tamsin considered before answering. 'He certainly

managed to charm Aunt Scott and that is quite a feat.'
But she did not add: you may well meet him soon, for he
has come to stay in the district.

That, she thought grimly, might prove a very interesting encounter for David St John, even if it caused Miss
Edgecombe some embarrassment. Tamsin determined
to hold fast to the knowledge that Mr St John was at best
a flirt, at worst a libertine. This intelligence, she told
herself sternly, must destroy her feelings for him . . . if
she had any sense of right or wrong.

Fortunately, Miss Edgecombe was too delighted to
have a sympathetic ear in which to pour her hopes for a
golden future with Mr James to pay much attention to
Tamsin's silent preoccupation with duty and emotion.

'I have been thinking, dearest,' she said earnestly,
which from experience Tamsin knew meant Miss Edgecombe had been working out some devious little
scheme, 'that as Sir Everard has already met my dearest
Elliot in Paris he might, on his return, be willing to help
him. His patronage could provide Elliot with all sorts of
introductions, which might lead to commissions for
portraits. I can't begin to tell you what a wonderful
painter he is, Tamsin. Please promise you will put in a
good word for him with your Sir Everard. He is bound to
listen to you . . .'

Tamsin could not imagine influencing Everard
Fortune to do anything, but if he had formed a good
opinion of Mr James it might carry sufficient weight with
Leonie's mamma and uncle to convince them that perhaps the young artist was not such an undesirable suitor
after all.

'Of course, I shall do my best for your sake,' Tamsin
promised, and wondered exactly when Everard would
arrive at Stillwater.

When, with many affectionate farewells, the young ladies parted they were agreeably surprised to discover their elders had decreed they might call on each other as often as they chose, and indeed it had already been arranged that Tamsin would visit Fairford again the following afternoon.

'Walking or driving without a chaperone in this rural area,' the rector had assured Tamsin's aunt, 'neither causes concern nor raises eyebrows.'

Since he possessed a governess cart which Miss Edgecombe was quite welcome to use, Mrs Scott need have no qualms about her niece driving one of the light equipages from Sir Everard's collection, particularly as Tamsin was well accustomed to driving to and from church in her small dog cart. The footpath connecting Fairford with Stillwater was less than two miles across the fields and Mrs Scott decided that such healthy exercise might also improve her niece's appetite and colour, both of which were too pallid even for that good lady's sense of maidenly modesty.

However much the rector might fulminate in private against Sir Everard's notorious style of living he could not ignore the prestige his niece, and by association he and his wife, must enjoy by being on the most friendly terms with the future mistress of Stillwater. The young Lady Fortune would not forget such close friends when composing invitation lists of notable local gentry . . .

From Leonie's wide, happy smile Tamsin knew all too well that the minx was making plans. Her uncle had just presented her with sufficient freedom and a plausible excuse for any amount of small excursions which meant that meetings with her best-beloved Mr James, whenever he appeared in the district, should not be too difficult to engineer.

The return journey to Stillwater took them back through St Adwyn. All was tranquil outside the Rising Sun so that Tamsin could almost believe her previous sighting of Mr St John had been a mere figment of a fevered imagination. By the time they re-entered the lodge gates, her head quite buzzed with Mrs Scott's accounts of the good deeds and righteous thoughts of Leonie's uncle and aunt. However, Tamsin could scarce refrain from laughing aloud for, despite the paragons' influence, their niece somehow remained just as much the devious butterfly as she was in her mamma's house.

She was glad to have the excuse of needing to run up to her room to remove her bonnet in order to escape Aunt Scott's monologue. Propped against the dressing-stand where she could not overlook it was one of Messrs de la Rue's gummed envelopes addressed to her in a hand she did not recognise, and indeed in one that looked as if its owner had some difficulty in mastering the art of writing. How it came there she could not imagine.

She rang the bell, and the maid who had been selected to wait upon her appeared almost instantly, bobbing a curtsy and giving a shy smile to the young lady the household were hoping would soon provide Stillwater with all the gaiety and excitement of guests, dances and hunting parties, and eventually with the sound of children's laughter. In the servants hall they were as unanimous of the suitability of Sir Everard's bride-to-be to make them an excellent mistress as were they on the less beguiling aspects of Aunt Scott.

Tamsin pointed at the envelope and enquired mildly: 'Who brought this, Mary?'

'While you were out visiting, miss, a lad from the village delivered it to one o' the gardeners who gave it to

an indoor servant. We were told it was to be given only
to you, so rather than hand it to you in front of your aunt
I put it where you'd be most likely to notice it.' She
added rather anxiously: 'I hope I did right.'

Tamsin smiled reassuringly and thanked her. When
the girl had gone she picked up the missive and turned it
over and over in her hands. It is the only letter I have
ever received that need not be read by Aunt Scott, she
thought wonderingly. How very pleasant it is to know
that every movement I make at Stillwater will not be
automatically reported to my aunt, although I presume
the servants will relay the arrival of this letter to their
master on his return.

She glanced out of her window at a view which had
already become very dear to her and sighed. Rolling
verdant lawns, the box-hedge maze, the formal rose
garden with a small stone summer-house at its centre
which had been the site of her last battle with Everard,
the glinting snake of river marked with eddying gold-
edged circles where trout rose to catch flies in the evening sun, the rustic footbridge, and beyond a dark copse,
green fields, and a distant spire pointing into a misty
heaven which twilight was shading a soft lilac. . . .

All this beauty belonged to an idyll of romance.

All this beauty would surround her for a lifetime if she
married a man who did not care for her and whom she
loathed. Now even that sour fact of life was made less
palatable because she had inadvertently given her heart
to another who neither knew nor sought such a boon. If
only the Fortune inheritance was not so desirable she
would not be quite so aware of the sharp difference
between her girlish dreams of love and the reality that
was to be hers.

Tamsin prised open the envelope and smoothed out

the enclosed sheet of paper to read:

'My dear Miss Lucas, I shall wait for you tomorrow morning at the ruined mill. To reach it, simply cross the footbridge and continue along the path for about a mile. I beg you to meet me there for I have matters of urgency to discuss with you. I shall wait all morning.'

It was signed: 'Your obedient servant, David St John.'

Her first reaction was astonishment. She would never have believed his handwriting could be so rough, almost illegible, especially when his cousin's was distinguished and elegant as befitted any gentleman of education. Mr St John's hand seemed to belong to his pedlar's disguise.

Her second reaction was one of acute suspicion. Was this the trap to be set on Everard's instructions?

Obviously the only way to avoid such a snare was to refuse to go anywhere near the ruined mill.

And yet . . .

For her heart could still whisper 'and yet . . .' It denied the caution urged by her brain, insisting it longed to see David St John just once more and this might be the last opportunity she would ever have to be alone with him. For on the morrow Sir Everard could well arrive. Besides, she could not abstain from curiosity. Just how would he explain his unheralded presence in the vicinity and his curious attire, and what matters of urgency did he wish to communicate to her?

Even as she determined to delay making any decision on whether or not to go to the mill until the morning Tamsin knew quite well what she would decide. . . .

The early morning dawned a hazy cornflower blue and promised to turn into a bright hot day. The exultant dawn chorus was replaced by a soft, languorous cooing of doves perched on their cote beyond the stableyard.

It was easier than she had imagined to remark to Aunt Scott: 'I think this morning I shall take a short walk along the footpath in the direction of Fairford to see if the way is very rough so I may decide whether to walk or drive there this afternoon. Would you care to accompany me, aunt?'

The question was posed casually and gave no hint of a heart which quaked lest Mrs Scott decide to ignore her troublesome feet and accept the invitation. Guiltily, Tamsin realised she was being just as cunning as Miss Edgecombe in using as a pretext for a clandestine rendezvous those legitimate visits to Fairford.

It seemed Leonie had not exaggerated when she had told her she, too, would not behave quite so properly if her heart were once involved.

Mrs Scott was contentedly devouring a Stillwater breakfast which was even more substantial than that offered by Connaught Square. In a voice somewhat distorted by a large mouthful of grilled trout she said: 'No, my dear, I shall stay here. I have informed Mrs Coles I intend to inspect her still-room this morning. By all means, have a good walk. I trust it will quicken your appetite for you have eaten nothing at all. Take care to wear your deepest-brimmed bonnet and carry a parasol, for I doubt Sir Everard will appreciate a fiancée as freckled and sunburned as a dairymaid.'

Tamsin did not express aloud her belief that she doubted if Sir Everard would appreciate her however she looked.

It was difficult to choose what to wear. While she wanted to look her best, commonsense dictated it would be foolish to put on one of Leonie's more elaborate gowns. At last, with the assistance of Mary who assured

Miss Lucas she looked very summery and countrified, 'Just right for a stroll in the gardens,' Tamsin donned a simple full-skirted cotton gown of blue, grey and white stripes. Its high-necked bodice and long, tight sleeves were edged with fine bands of blue lace. The coal-scuttle straw bonnet tied beneath her chin with matching blue ribbons. Tamsin thought she seemed very much more the dairymaid than a fashionable lady affianced to Sir Everard Fortune, and wondered wistfully if Mr St John preferred simplicity to high fashion.

In case the walk took longer than expected the 'dairymaid' tucked beneath her arm a sketch book and colours so that any delay might be blamed on a pretty scene she had stopped to copy.

It was a small, demure figure that tripped across the lawn in the direction of the river with a parasol tilted slightly against her right shoulder. The feet tapping on the wooden footbridge echoed the hammering of her heart. Once amid the shadows of the copse she knew she was out of sight of curious eyes which might be observing Miss Lucas's progress from Stillwater's windows. As she had not been able to see the ruined mill from her own window Tamsin could safely assume it was round a bend and therefore invisible from the house.

The footpath was somewhat overgrown although not too rough for her light leather pumps. She suspected it was not used regularly which was all to the good, for she did not want some ploughboy to happen upon Sir Everard's future wife in tête-à-tête with his cousin. What a topic of gossip that would provide in the local taverns!

From a distance the mill did not seem derelict. Only when she drew closer did she see the millstone had not turned for a long time and the walls of the little stone bridge, which spanned the tributary of the river, were upholstered in moss.

Standing with his face averted from her, gazing into the distance, was Mr St John. He appeared lost in thought and looked almost sad.

Tamsin noticed a fairly heavy wicker hamper pushed against the side of the ruined building and Mr St John was evidently overheated from his exertions of carrying it there for he had thrown aside hat, coat and waistcoat, and even undone his silk cravat. His full-sleeved white shirt was open at the throat to reveal a sun-tanned neck, and his hair, usually so carefully curled, looked as if he had but recently run his fingers through it. In this disarray David St John seemed younger and less worldly than in formal attire.

Tamsin paused to compose herself. In an effort to stop her heart fluttering as wildly as a caged bird trying to escape its prison she took several deep breaths. Never before had she seen any gentleman so casually dressed.

'Good . . . good day, Mr St John,' her voice was as flustered as her feelings.

He turned immediately towards her and his dark eyes seemed to fill with sunlight.

'My dear Miss Lucas, how delighted I am you accepted my somewhat informal invitation. I feared you would not. How pretty you are—perfectly in tune with this glorious summer morning. Only,' he added in an anxious tone, 'you seem pale and tired after your walk. Come, sit down here.' He patted the low wall, and placed his coat over it to shield her gown against the moss.

Tamsin coloured but sank down gratefully. At breakfast she had had no appetite but now the walk had left her both thirsty and hungry.

As if he divined these feelings, Mr St John said: 'I believe I have here just the thing to revive you.'

He knelt beside the millstream and retrieved a glistening dark green bottle from the water where it had been wedged upright between two stones.

'It is not a marvellous wine,' he admitted, 'but the best the inn could offer when I asked for something liquid to accompany the cold collation they had prepared.'

He rummaged in the hamper and withdrew two glasses which he filled with a pale golden liquid, and handed one of them to Tamsin.

'Your health, Miss Lucas,' he said and sipped his wine.

Tamsin looked at her glass uncertainly, but thirst triumphed over all her aunt's advice against eating and drinking in the open, and she swallowed some of the cool, slightly perfumed wine.

It tasted better than anything she had ever drunk.

'You would be much more comfortable without that wretched parasol and bonnet,' he remarked practically, removing the sunshade from her hand and laying it beside the hamper.

'I . . . I must not get my skin sunburned,' she protested.

'A little colour will become that pale face,' he returned easily.

There was something about the strength of character Mr St John exuded which made it impossible for Tamsin to argue with him. Reluctantly, she undid the ribbons at her chin and removed the bonnet. She must have disturbed the pins securing her chignon for in a trice the hair had escaped to cascade about her shoulders, causing her to blush with crimson confusion, for Aunt Scott had said no gentleman, save a husband or a close relative, should see a lady with her hair undone.

With gentle fingers Mr St John pushed the hair back from her face.

'You may put it up after we have eaten,' he said cheerfully, and then in a different and vibrant tone: 'Did nobody ever tell you you have hair like a goddess? It should always be worn loose to show off its beauty and not confined to the formal dictates of fashion.'

'I fear my aunt would scarcely agree with you,' Tamsin smiled up at him. She was overwhelmed by her feelings, for while she felt vulnerable in his company she also felt curiously safe.

Mr St John returned to the hamper and produced a white linen serviette containing some fresh pasties which he offered to Tamsin.

She took one, confessing: 'I am quite hungry,' and began to eat with more relish than her aunt had recommended might be properly demonstrated by a modest young female in masculine company.

'You look as if you have not been eating sufficiently,' observed Mr St John, his even teeth biting deep into a pasty which he chewed with evident enjoyment.

Somehow his drawing-room manners had been cast aside with coat and waistcoat to reveal a much more honest, down-to-earth fellow. The sort, Tamsin reflected, who would not mind getting his hands dirty if there was some essential task to be tackled. It made him appear stronger, and more reliable, and she found it harder to hold to her suspicions of him being an untrustworthy rake bent on making mischief for his cousin's benefit.

'Is the food at Stillwater not to your liking?' he demanded.

'It is very fine. I haven't felt very hungry of late.'

'You are worried over something. I can see it. Anxiety clouds your eyes like a storm gathering far out at sea. Will you not confide your problem to me? Perhaps I may be of help.'

Her eyes great with apprehension, Tamsin stared at this gentleman who possessed the uncanny power of looking deep into her mind.

Her sudden outburst of slightly bitter laughter startled him so that the dark brows drew together, creasing his forehead in a puzzled frown.

'You are one person to whom I dare not voice my problems,' she said, and laid aside the half-eaten pasty for her appetite had vanished.

'I thought you regarded me as a friend . . . Tamsin . . .' It was the first time he had spoken her name, and he pronounced it lingeringly so that it almost sounded like an endearment.

'I beg your pardon. *Miss Lucas*. But, I think of you as Tamsin.' He grinned wickedly. 'Hardly ever as Thomasina unless you are being specially provoking!'

'Do you think of me?' she asked, wanting to know, while wondering at the propriety of putting such a question.

'Can you doubt it?'

'I suppose you do so in order to obey your cousin's instructions,' she said levelly, determined to drive away those feelings his tender enquiry evoked.

'I think of you in order to please myself, miss,' he retorted. 'Must you attribute everything I do to Everard Fortune?'

Defiantly, Tamsin raised her chin and shook back her hair. Had he not lured her there for Everard's sake? 'Of course.'

'Well, Miss Lucas, you are utterly wrong!' Now, the

tenderness had fled his voice; it was almost savage. 'But, I imagine you are thinking in terms of pleasing this absent gentleman who will have everything to offer you once he has given you his name.'

Two tears rose unbidden to her eyes and overflowed to roll down her cheeks. She brushed them away with impatient fingers.

'What the devil have I said to cause you to weep?' he demanded, refusing to let her tears soften his attitude.

'Oh, you do not understand me.' Unhappiness transformed her gentle voice into a wail of protest.

'I understand you perfectly, miss,' his words had a cruel edge to them. 'You are like most other young ladies, although I had genuinely believed—and hoped— you might belong to a different breed. Now you have seen the Connaught Square house and Stillwater you are determined to become Lady Fortune, are you not, whatever your heart may whisper to you. All you want is a title and as much wealth as possible. The nature of the husband who provides these perquisites is of little account.' He seemed to take pleasure in goading her to reveal her innermost thoughts.

So tormented was she by this indictment that Tamsin all but shouted: 'I do not want to marry Everard Fortune at all!'

Then, realising what she had just confessed, her hands flew to cover the lower part of her face while she stared at him with horrified eyes.

'Why?' he probed, apparently unperturbed by her admission. 'So that he will not come into his father's inheritance? Would that not prove to be a case of cutting off your pretty nose to spite your charming face? Whatever Everard forfeited by your refusal to wed him would be small compared with your own loss. I believe you have no money of your own, whereas he still has a trifle left from his mamma and I imagine would not find it too difficult to marry the daughter of some rich industrialist willing to barter wealth for a connection with an old titled family.'

Tamsin nodded soberly. Now she had uttered such self-condemnatory words there was scant point in disguising her true material situation with small social untruths.

'My father's will bequeathed me nothing but instructions to marry Everard when I attained my eighteenth birthday and entrust my future to the Fortune sense of fair-play. Since Sir Oliver had won so much of papa's money at cards he seemed to imagine I had a justifiable claim to a share of Everard's inheritance. Apparently, Sir Oliver approved this view, hence his will.

'No doubt,' she continued pensively, 'by requiring me to marry at eighteen they believed there would be insufficient time for me to form some undesirable romantic attachment before Everard and I were united.' Silently, she added: how wrong they were!

'If I forego my chance to become Lady Fortune Aunt Scott sees little hope of me marrying without a dowry. I expect I shall have to earn my living as a governess.'

Tamsin stared at the dark shapes of trout flitting below the limpid waters of the millstream. 'I may as well confess I did toy with the idea of not marrying your cousin for the problems it must cause him. Yet, at the same time I realised I had no sensible alternative but to become his wife, and I had been brought up to regard that as a duty which must be done. I suppose,' she said wearily, 'you will report to him what I have just confessed.'

He shrugged. 'Why should I? Whatever else he is, Everard is not a fool. All the while he strove to find some way to nullify the conditions of his father's ridiculous testament he jested he would look the jobbernowl should Miss Lucas cry off first. He has never imagined you nursed romantic feelings for his person, but presumed you would choose to marry him for wealth and position. It appears his judgment of your character was unsound.'

'I did not know he would think like that.'

'But you do not know Everard,' Mr St John reminded her reasonably. 'I assume you still recall a most indulged and precocious schoolboy while he remembers only a tiny pugnacious girl.'

She nodded. 'And now I have a reason more valid than pique for not wishing to become his wife . . .'

'Which is?' he prompted.

She would not answer, but examined her upturned palms as if seeking to read in them how her own impetuous words must irrevocably destroy the future that had been planned for her.

'Because you have fallen in love with another.'

No words of hers were required to confirm his quiet assertion, for the colour that flared refused to die away and she had to bury her telltale face against her arms to escape his probing eyes.

'You would give up everything—title, estates, money—for this love?' he demanded inexorably.

'Yes,' she said in a muffled voice.

'Then I trust the gentleman you love realises the sacrifices you are prepared to make for his sake. He is most honoured.'

Tamsin thought: you cannot know the irony of your words. If he has lured me here at Everard's behest in an effort to destroy my reputation he has succeeded all too admirably, and with my own foolish co-operation. I have presented him with the best ammunition Everard could ask for to rid himself of me and yet retain his inheritance. His lawyers are unlikely to insist he marry a girl who has admitted herself to be in love with another. That admission must render me totally unsuitable according to any of the terms Sir Oliver had stipulated for overturning the conditions of his will.

Worse still, was the knowledge that the man she loved would be bringing about her ruin without realising or caring whom she loved so long as the fact served to free his cousin. Of course, he did not return her love. Why should he?

'Drink some wine, Tamsin,' David St John commanded.

She peeped through her fingers to discover to her relief he was no longer watching her but gazing instead into the stream, chewing furiously at his lower lip as if he wrestled with an insoluble problem—or his conscience.

The wine gradually calmed her although it could not abate her misery. She waited in silence while he drank, thinking, he has me in his absolute power: my good name, my happiness, even my future way of life are dependent on what he chooses to tell his cousin.

Eventually, Mr St John set down his empty glass and, whistling cheerfully between his teeth, started to walk up and down and survey her from various angles much as he might view an inanimate piece of sculpture.

'Pray, sir, what are you about?' she demanded sharply, quite forgetting that only a moment before he had witnessed her guilty discomfiture and she was scarcely in any position to play the indignant maiden.

'I am about composing a photograph of you, Miss Lucas,' he returned, 'which is one of my motives for asking you to meet me in this picturesque but unfrequented spot. I have the equipment I need in that hamper, and devilish heavy it was toting it here.'

'A photograph for Sir Everard?'

He grinned impudently. 'What! Show him his future wife with her hair hanging down her back like any milk-maid! Would that not be most improper, Miss Lucas?' he teased. 'I am sure your aunt has informed you how unseemly it is for a lady to be seen with her hair loose by any gentleman other than a close relative. No, *I* wish to retain a memento of how you look today for myself.'

'I shall put my hair up this instant,' she said stiffly, and began a frantic search for pins and combs.

'No, you won't. I am the photographer and I know what I require of the model I choose. Leave your hair as it is with the sun shining on it to produce a halo effect.'

So, she thought grimly, he will have incontestable evidence to show Sir Everard how abandoned and there-fore unworthy to be his future wife is Miss Thomasina Kate Lucas.

Deftly, Mr St John began to unpack the contents of the hamper, and she watched him assemble various pieces of what she recognised from the Exhibition to be photographic equipment.

'But you will have to look a lot happier than that,' he called over his shoulder. 'Wistful, yes, but not woebegone.'

No longer did he bother to play the respectful caller who had bent his ear to Aunt Scott's slightest opinion. Now he was an autocratic teacher.

She started violently when he returned to her side to place his hands upon her shoulders, half turning her away from him.

'My dear girl, will you be still.' His tone was quite irritated, 'I merely wish to place you in a correct attitude. Do not wriggle like a fish upon a hook. Cup your chin in that hand, so, and hold this bluebell loosely with the other.'

Despite herself, Tamsin began to giggle.

She half looked up at his stern features to remark impishly: 'Mr St John, you have the manner of a schoolmaster.'

'Only when dealing with a young lady who behaves like a foolish schoolgirl,' he retorted, 'but now his eyes were laughing. 'Kindly hold that pose until I give you permission to move. If you stir before then you will quite ruin my work and I shall be exceedingly angry. It is not often I have precisely the sunlight that is required for a photograph, so we must take full advantage of it,' he told her firmly before disappearing under the dark, voluminous cloth which partially concealed him and the camera.

She sat there without moving for what felt like an age, unaware that a small smile hovered about her lips. Although this was the first time she had ever had her image captured by the camera Tamsin found that, instead of nervously concentrating upon being still, she was thinking how, although they had spent but little time together, and there were so many tangible reasons separating them, a strange bond appeared to exist between them.

Was it the camaraderie of brother and sister? No, perhaps not that, she decided, for although she had neither brother nor sister, Tamsin sensed the link between Mr St John and herself was of another nature. It seemed almost incredible that not many minutes beforehand tension and confusion had reigned over them. Now, so intent was Mr St John behind the camera that he appeared to have forgotten all about her lamentable confession and ascendancy it gave him and Everard over her. . . .

'You may move as much as you like now, even dance a jig if you should so wish,' he called out cheerfully, re-emerging from beneath the cloth. 'I believe I have achieved a most effective study which I shall entitle "Beauty beside the Mill". But,' he added airily, 'unless you give me leave I do not think I shall exhibit this to your Aunt Scott who might swoon upon the spot from one glance at it.'

Laughing because she understood he teased her, Tamsin stood up to stretch her cramped limbs.

'But you have not yet told me what it is you wish so urgently to communicate,' she reminded him.

'I wonder you have not already guessed,' he said, seeming to focus his attention on dismantling and re-packing the photographic equipment.

She shook her head without comprehension.

There was a long pause while he fastened the straps on the hamper. Then, he came towards her to stand so close that she felt his breath upon her cheek and once more inhaled the aroma of macassar oil. Gently, he placed both hands upon her shoulders so she could not move away and said in a voice which brooked no refusal: 'Tamsin, look at me.'

She obeyed, wishing she did not always begin to tremble at his touch.

'Do you really not know what it is I wish to say to you?'

She shook her head uncertainly, so that her cape of hair was a glistening waterfall about her shoulders and breasts. 'Has it to do with Everard?'

Mr St John emitted a most exasperated snort of laughter.

'Thomasina Kate Lucas, you are the most provoking

girl! I quite despair of your perspicacity, and I had begun to have a high opinion of your intellect when we visited the Exhibition for you asked the most intelligent questions. Oh, I understand it is not fashionable for ladies to know anything, but life could be a little tedious in the company of someone who is devoid of both intelligence and curiosity. Yet, now you have the audacity to plead ignorance of something which is only too obvious.'

'I . . . I don't understand,' she whispered dismayed. 'Please, what is it you want me to know?'

'This,' he said roughly.

Without any warning he crushed her in his arms, pouring kisses on her upturned face. His lips brushed her eyelids, her cheeks and even her ear lobes, but they lingered above her mouth as if enticing it to respond to his passion.

Then, in a breathless almost angry voice, he demanded: 'Do you not realise I adore you, Tamsin, and I am hoping the man you admit to loving is me? If he is not, by Heaven I swear I shall horsewhip the scoundrel and hold you prisoner until you learn to love me . . .'

And his tone was only half bantering.

'I did not know,' she said wonderingly. 'Can you really care for me?'

In reply he pressed his mouth firmly against hers and this time Tamsin did not struggle to escape but returned his kiss with an ardour she had no idea she possessed. Her arms entwined about him as if their owner could not stand without his support.

'You will think me a shameless creature,' she protested weakly, 'but I cannot help myself when you hold me so close.'

'My precious, precious girl,' he whispered tenderly.

'Did I not tell you you were made for love?'

So he had not forgotten those words she was unable to obliterate from her memory.

David St John stroked her soft tresses, murmuring: 'How much I do love you, Tamsin.'

'When did it begin?' she asked, scarcely able to believe his declaration.

He drew her to the bridge where they sat side by side on the wall overlooking the water, his arm about her waist. 'I think I must have fallen in love with you that night in the conservatory when I looked upon your lovely face,' he replied quietly. 'And then I was quite certain of my feelings when I glimpsed you the following day at the opening of the Exhibition.

'I have always been too much the man-of-the-world to advocate the romantics' philosophy of "love born at first sight" and yet it has happened to me. But I had no idea of your name or where you lived or even if you were already betrothed.

'Imagine my ecstasy—and consternation—when I discovered the young lady I was bound to contact was none other than the one I most longed to find in the whole of London. How kind fate was to me for once, and I have always named her a fickle jade!'

'David . . .' she tried the name aloud, although she had whispered it soundlessly to herself. 'David . . .' and she savoured the name as if it were the rarest fruit of which she could never have sufficient.

'But, dear miss, you have not yet told me if I am the one you love. Perhaps I am taking too much for granted by my assumption that I am he.'

She lowered her eyelids and David St John placed an unyielding finger beneath her chin which forced her to look up at him as she answered.

'Yes, I do love you . . . very much . . . I fear,' she murmured, and then buried her face against his chest, feeling the heat of his flesh emanate from beneath the fine linen shirt.

'Why do you fear it?' he laughed.

'Because of what a sad muddle and scandal it will cause,' she responded gravely.

'What muddle? What scandal?' His tone suggested genuine surprise so she stared at him in amazement. Had he forgotten how and why they had ever met?

'Because of Everard.'

'Damn Everard!' he exclaimed cheerfully.

'David,' her voice was reproachful. 'Do you not think he will be angered to discover how his future wife and the cousin, acting as his envoy, have fallen in love with each other? I should imagine he can be very arrogant, especially if he feels himself thwarted. He may not want to marry me, but I doubt he will like to be made to look a fool in the eyes of the world. He might retaliate by making some dreadful scandal . . . or . . .' she added a little diffidently, 'refusing to help you in any way, for you have intimated that he has given you financial assistance.'

David St John appeared to ponder her words for a moment, and then shrugged carelessly, as if to rid himself of their sense. 'We shall cross that bridge when we reach it, dear one. But, look at the sun. It is past noon. You should hurry back to Stillwater before Mrs Scott grows alarmed.'

She began to put up her hair, looking to the stream to serve as an impromptu looking-glass. He thought what a charming pastoral scene it made: few men were privileged to see a lady doing her hair in natural surroundings.

With a voice slightly impaired by a mouthful of pins, she asked: 'Will you not escort me back to Stillwater, dearest?' and she blushed to use this endearment for the first time. 'We can always explain to aunt that we chanced to meet on the footpath. I know she will be happy to see you, and . . .' Could he divine just how studied was her careless tone? 'Learn how you came to be in this district so soon after our own arrival. You could leave that hamper here and collect it on your return. Then, we would be together for longer . . .'

He shook his head. 'No, sweetheart, I fear you must go back alone, for I don't think it would be wise for me to be seen at Stillwater, especially by the Fortune servants.'

'Why ever not?' she asked, and re-tied the bonnet strings, hoping the effect would not suggest to sharp eyes they had been arranged without the aid of a dressing-mirror.

'You must know I only came to this neighbourhood to be near to you, but it was without first seeking Everard's permission. Since he did not request me to escort you and Mrs Scott to Stillwater he clearly intended me to remain in London, which is why I have chosen to stay quietly in the village, where I try not to draw too much attention to my presence by wearing over-fashionable clothes, though I suspect the good folk at the inn are mightily intrigued by my trunks of photographic equipment. I doubt Everard would like me to visit his house without him inviting me and the servants are bound to tell him if I call upon you.'

The water reflected his brooding countenance. 'You are right about my cousin being something of an auto-crat, my love. He likes his own way in all things. We should do nothing to offend him until we have decided what is to be done with the future.'

'Whatever you say, David,' Tamsin was submissive but a little disappointed.

He gave her a careful kiss upon the cheek which could not disarrange bonnet or hair, and handed her back the parasol and sketching pad. 'Where will you be this afternoon, Tamsin?'

'I am driving over to Fairford, and . . .' Her face glowed with happiness at a sudden notion. 'If you just happened to be walking along that road I should be delighted to drive you a short way, even if Aunt Scott were with me. You need only tell her that you are passing through this area. That would not seem suspicious so long as you appeared vastly surprised to meet us.'

'What a charming conspirator you would make, dear heart,' he chuckled. 'Very well, I shall hate all the minutes until we are re-united on the Fairford road. Now, be off with you.'

He stood watching as she picked her way along the footpath, halting every few yards to turn and wave to him.

Tamsin was a little piqued that even before she was out of sight he had ceased to look after her but was hurriedly collecting his belongings, as if he had to attend to urgent business.

Only when she reached the shadow of the copse did her haze of joy begin to evaporate to reveal the harsh facts of the situation which now existed. A troubled frown replaced her dreamy smile.

David may indeed love you, she told herself despondently, but he has said nothing of marriage. Nor may he crave a penniless wife, especially as Everard is unlikely to offer him any further help when the truth is known.

Thought of Everard Fortune brought with it apprehension. That she loved his cousin and was loved in return could not avert a confrontation with him as well as Aunt Scott, which might involve her own humiliation and disgrace—without necessarily the healing reward of future bliss in the arms of David St John.

And, while David had given reasons for his covert arrival in the district as well as his ruffianly clothes Tamsin could not avoid feeling that a mystery remain. If the man she adored kept secrets from her, dare she trust him completely?

CHAPTER
SEVEN

SUNLIGHT filtering down through the leaves dappled the narrow road to Fairford with patches of light and shade. The reins lay easily in her hands as the grey horse trotted smartly along the quiet way. There were no other vehicles, and only in the village fording the stream where David St John was lodging were there a few men standing outside the inn, and some women with children at their skirts doing the laundry at the village pump.

The shawled and bonneted young lady driving sedately through the village attracted only passing curiosity.

As the horse's hooves clipped against loose stones Tamsin realised her somewhat breathless feelings could be attributed to pangs of conscience as well as anticipation.

It seemed she was possessed of a cunning equal to Miss Edgecombe's, or perhaps when circumstances required it even the most properly-reared young lady might behave in a less than creditable manner. By dint of encouraging her aunt's appetite at luncheon she had assured herself of Mrs Scott being far too sleepy even to contemplate accompanying her to Fairford. She needed only slight prompting from Tamsin to do her duty and help herself to gargantuan samples of at least three entrées, including young rabbit stuffed with prunes and forcemeat, the leg of a guinea fowl, and a thick slice of saddle of mutton in caper sauce, to say nothing of various vegetables and other side dishes. All this was followed by a selection of delicate cold desserts as well as a robust hot pippin tart.

Between mouthfuls Mrs Scott had spent the meal regaling Tamsin with a precise account of the contents of the stillroom, the pantries and all the other cupboards she had browbeaten Mrs Coles into allowing her to inspect, so she had little breath or curiosity left to enquire too closely into her niece's morning walk. While she was pleased to note a delicate colour bloomed in the girl's cheeks Aunt Scott much deplored the still absent appetite . . . as well as the fact she had been unable to fault the management of Stillwater!

Not even the appearance of rose-petal flavoured jelly and cinnamon ice-cream could entice Tamsin. For that half-consumed pasty and the knowledge of David St John's love, with the attendant obstacles, ensured she had no room for food however delicious.

While she might derive a slight sense of triumph in besting Aunt Scott Tamsin felt more guilty about the consideration shown her by the grooms and stablehands. Evidently, Sir Everard had instructed his household to treat Miss Lucas as if she were already their mistress so that when she hesitantly asked for some light equipage to drive herself the request was immediately granted in the shape of an elegant little phaeton drawn by a thoroughbred mare. The most dashing London beauty would have counted herself fortunate to be seen driving it in Hyde Park and Tamsin knew with a swift twinge of complacency that Leonie Edgecombe would be turned quite green with envy at sight of it.

All these unexpected kindnesses of Everard's—albeit by proxy—will make the situation between us the more fraught when eventually he arrives at Stillwater, she reflected with a heavy heart. By making me welcome at two of his homes he appears to have given up trying to rid himself of his unwanted bride and is endeavouring to behave towards me in a way society will deem as acceptable.

But when he discovers my perfidy he can quite justifiably accuse me of exploiting his hospitality. It is a poor excuse to claim I have fallen in love with his cousin, for what has love to do with the duty Aunt Scott has taught me is mine to fulfil? And she shuddered as she considered what harm his anger could inflict on the lovers who had made him look ridiculous.

If only he had continued to ignore my existence, or behave in the thoroughly boorish fashion I would have expected of him, I should not now be feeling quite so wretched. . . .

She had not travelled many yards beyond the village precincts when a tall gentleman, immaculate in dark blue with a grey top hat and sporting a malacca cane, stepped jauntily into her path.

Tamsin halted the unprotesting horse, and said in a calm voice which belied the wild beating of her heart: 'Why, Mr St John, what a pleasant surprise. I happen to be driving towards Fairford. Perhaps you would care to accompany me in that direction.'

Her expression was one of demure friendliness as might properly be shown to any gentleman of her aunt's acquaintance, and gave no hint of her passionate longing to throw herself into his arms and have him kiss her lips until she almost swooned of love.

'My dear Miss Lucas,' he mimicked her tone and theatrically laid a hand upon his heart. 'How kind of you.'

Laughing, he sprang up beside her, his hand stealing boldly about her waist.

'What a wicked little creature you are, and how I adore you for it! I am astonished and gratified to discover Miss Lucas is not quite the prim maiden Mrs Scott would have her be,' he remarked, drawing her close and kissing her cheek.

'You must not do that,' she protested scandalised, and pulled away from his embrace. 'Someone might see us.'

David St John grinned unrepentantly. 'Ah, but I may do so when there is no one around to see, eh my love?'

Tamsin blushed and tossed her head. Now his behaviour was reminiscent of the philanderer in the conservatory rather than the lover who had declared himself to her that morning. However, he patted her gloved fingers reassuringly and then, with ostentatious politeness, placed his own hands upon his knees while she urged the horse into a trot.

They drove without speaking, but stealing little sideways glances at him, Tamsin deduced David St John to be in a mighty good mood, for he kept smiling to himself as if he possessed some secret which he had difficulty in keeping.

She had no wish to mar his good humour but was anxious they discuss with all possible haste her fears of Everard's reaction to their love.

'Dearest,' she began, 'we simply must talk of . . .'

But she did not have a chance to tell him the topic she had chosen for coming towards them was a figure she knew only too well.

Miss Edgecombe, evidently out for an innocent afternoon's promenade and no doubt hoping to encounter her friend driving over from Stillwater, strolled slowly along the lane, twirling a black fringed, white silken parasol.

Very stylish she looked, too, in a black and white

corded silk gown with a white silk bonnet trimmed with
nodding black flowers. This exceptionally becoming outfit belonged in Bond Street rather than a rural back-
water, and as she walked listening to the pleasing swish
of silk against muslin petticoats, Leonie glanced from
side to side in case the hedgerows contained rustic
bystanders who might welcome the opportunity of
admiring the progress of a London belle. She was in
marvellously good spirits and could almost have hugged
herself with happiness.

On the other hand, Tamsin was quite downcast, and
could have kicked herself for being such an unwitting
fool. When she suggested meeting David St John on this
road she had not thought of the possibility of meeting
Leonie, for she had intended to let him descend before
they entered Fairford. Now there was nothing she could
do to prevent Mr St John from renewing his acquaintance with the original owner of the rose-coloured ball
gown, and it might be that whatever flame of passion had
flickered at Baden Baden would be rekindled. . . .

Understandably, Miss Edgecombe's attention was
much diverted by the approaching phaeton. She noticed
it was driven by a lady, and quite envied the female who
had the occasion to cut such a dash, but she did not
associate this stylish light carriage with her dutiful friend,
Miss Lucas. For an instant, she envisaged herself holding the reins of a similar vehicle, wearing exactly the
right sort of costume, of course, something blue and
tailored like a riding-habit she rather thought. . . .

Suddenly the driver's bonnet and gown recommended
themselves to Miss Edgecombe's somewhat haphazard
memory, which was scarcely surprising as she had only
recently passed them on to Tamsin. Impatiently, she
waited for the phaeton to draw level and stop, and then

had the dilemma of deciding which first to devour with her eyes: the marvellous carriage or the handsome, though extremely serious, bearded gentleman.

'My dearest Tamsin,' cried Leonie, 'I so longed to see you that I told Mamma and Aunt Sophronia I simply had to come to meet you along the road. How perfectly splendid you look. You quite put Uncle Septimus's old governess cart and broken-down nag to shame. I shall be too embarrassed to drive to Stillwater to visit you.' She smiled expectantly towards the gentleman and waited to be introduced.

Initially she had assumed that here was Everard Fortune arrived home, yet she had never seen him, but felt quite certain this gentleman was somebody she had met . . . although where and when she could not tell. She thought there must be something different about him. But what? The effort of trying to recall his identity and how he might have changed quite wrinkled her brow.

'How lovely you look, as always,' Tamsin's voice was rather flat. 'But you should not have walked along this dusty road in that splendid gown. Pray allow me to introduce you to Mr St John—Sir Everard's cousin—of whom I have already spoken. We . . . we met quite by chance along the road and I offered to drive him a short distance . . .' Knowing that Miss Edgecombe would scarcely keep silent about this encounter she added swiftly: 'Unexpected business brings him to this part of the world which is why I am so amazed to see him . . .' She considered her explanation sounded lame, but Leonie was too absorbed in her contemplation of David St John to question the veracity of her friend's words.

'Mr St John, may I present my dearest friend, Miss Edgecombe.'

Leonie was quite surprised at how cold Tamsin's tone had become.

Nimbly, David St John jumped down to bow over Leonie's gloved hand. Tamsin noticed that he bit back a somewhat rueful grin, and thought grimly: ah, so now he understands the riddle of that familiar ball gown and guesses I wear Miss Edgecombe's cast-offs, but he cannot believe me so much the love-blinded simpleton as not to realise the full implication of his behaviour in the conservatory.

'I am sure we have met before, Mr St John,' Leonie said archly, putting her head to one side in a pretty, puzzled gesture. 'Although I vow I have only heard your name since sweet Tamsin and my Mamma mentioned you in connection with Sir Everard.'

Feeling anything but sweet, Tamsin waited to see how he would deal with this situation.

'How could I forget your charming face, Miss Edgecombe?' David St John drawled gallantly. 'Of course we have met. In Baden Baden. What a pity I had to leave before we had exchanged names. Did I not stand beside you at one of the gaming-tables? If my memory serves me correct you helped me lose money I could ill afford. I could not blame you for it since you had first declared you knew nothing about gambling. But I had hoped you would bring me what is called beginner's luck. It is a small world, is it not?' he appealed to Tamsin, whose features were inflexibly unsmiling. 'You probably failed to recognise me because I have only recently grown this beard. You must tell Miss Lucas how I look without it.'

While he was speaking Miss Edgecombe's delicate colour had deepened to a most eloquent scarlet.

That beard had certainly altered his appearance. He

was as handsome—if not more so—but different.

Of course, she could remember the gentleman from the gaming-room now. Had he not escorted her out on to the terrace for some air and gaily demanded she reimburse him for his losses? Oh, she knew he had been teasing her for he was too much the gentleman to insist. But when she had apologised for having no money in her reticule, he had coolly returned: 'There are other ways a lady may settle her debts which I should find vastly more agreeable . . .'

And so she had been rash and let him make love to her. After all, no one in England need ever know. Her cousins were somewhat boring and she had hoped this worldly stranger would bring a little excitement to her sojourn at Baden Baden while she waited to return home to dear Mr James. Naturally, she had been disappointed not to see him again after that romantic interlude on the moonlit terrace for she had thought he might become a regular escort, but she had dared not show too much curiosity when trying to discover his name or where he might be staying in case her cousins grew suspicious and wrote to her mamma. Certainly, she had never imagined her peccadillo would find her out on the road to Fairford, of all places. Anxiously, she glanced at Miss Lucas and prayed Sir Everard's cousin would not confide this indiscretion to her.

'You must tell your mamma that Mr St John is already known to you,' Tamsin remarked. 'She will be so surprised.' Turning towards the gentleman, whom she trusted was suffering a few embarrassing moments, she added: 'You did not realise you knew Mrs Edgecombe's daughter, did you?'

His only reply was a curt shake of the head, for he was too astute not to realise that Tamsin must have long been aware of him having had some encounter with Miss Edgecombe.

Leonie did not look at all happy at her friend's proposal. 'Of course,' she murmured, 'however, please do not mention the gaming-room to mamma or Uncle Septimus. They would disapprove.'

'My lips are quite sealed on that subject,' Mr St John assured her. 'But I must take up no more of your time, ladies. I am sure you have much to talk of that will only be hampered by the presence of a mere male. Besides, I have an appointment.' He bowed towards Tamsin, and, with a formal smile, added: 'I am obliged to you, Miss Lucas, for driving me this far. Do remember me to your aunt. Your servant, Miss Edgecombe.'

Both young ladies watched in silence as he strode purposefully in the direction from whence he had just been driven. Neither of them commented how odd it was' he had agreed to ride with Tamsin when he had an appointment in an opposite direction.

Miss Edgecombe knew only relief that Mr St John had given no sign of any intimacy between them and concluded he was a perfect gentleman.

Miss Lucas, however, thought sorrowfully that only a true rake would be able to wear such an innocent face in the company of two ladies whose affections he had trifled with.

At length, she asked Leonie: 'Can you manage to climb up beside me?'

Somewhat inelegantly, Miss Edgecombe scrambled into the seat recently vacated by David St John. She picked up the tiny chased silver mirror suspended by a ribbon from her waist and began to examine her face for some invisible speck of dust—a gesture intended to calm her confusion.

'You never mentioned meeting such a charming person at Baden Baden.'

'It must have quite slipped my memory,' Leonie said untruthfully. For she was unlikely to forget the stranger's embraces, so different from Mr James's halting attempts at lovemaking. 'We spent only a few minutes together. I do believe someone did point him out to me as a gentleman who loves to flirt with the ladies. A regular Don Juan,' she giggled. 'But in that, I suppose he resembles his cousin.' She added carelessly: 'Did mamma not mention that Mr St John is quite without money of his own?'

Tamsin nodded.

'Ah well,' Leonie could be philosophical. Had he some of his cousin's expectations her interest in him might well have revived. 'I expect some young lady of means will entice him into matrimony. Of course, my dear Elliot is poor, but he would not marry for money— or flirt for the fun of it.' It was of comfort to her that Mr James's inexpert kisses suggested he had not had much experience at love. 'And, besides,' she added with a wisdom which was not usually apparent in her, 'a gentleman like Mr St John would prove very difficult for a wife to govern, unlike my best-beloved. A girl needs a reliable gentleman as a husband—unless he is very rich, of course. . . .'

And Tamsin could not dispute this fact.

How can I be sure he is not flirting with me as he did with Leonie and every other young female he has chanced upon, she demanded of herself. If he is a true libertine might he not even be pretending love for me on his cousin's instructions, and for financial reward, to provoke a scandal which would release Everard by showing me to be a shameless creature quite unfitted for the honourable attentions of any gentleman?

Such a notion fitted in much more with her long-held image of Everard Fortune, the ruthless, self-interested deceiver, rather than the suddenly thoughtful, though absent, host who had commanded his household to look only to Miss Lucas's comfort.

In the knowledge of his probable behaviour with Leonie how could she have permitted herself to fall in love with David St John? Why, oh why, had she chosen to ignore this blatant fact until it was too late? For the repercussion of those breathless, ecstatic moments spent in his arms could be much graver than anything Leonie might have faced in Baden Baden. . . .

Had not Miss Edgecombe been at her side Tamsin would have thrown herself on to a grassy bank to weep in despair.

The topic of Mr St John pushed aside, Leonie said breathlessly: 'Now I may tell you why I really hurried to meet you, dearest. I have such wonderful news. I have actually seen my Elliot. He arrived this morning and is staying just outside Fairford in a tiny inn on this very road.' She added dubiously: 'It is not a very elegant place, but he insists that economy must be his prime consideration.

'We have exchanged only a few words and . . .' she coloured prettily, 'a kiss or two. I have told him how we may meet daily for when I am not driving over to see you I shall certainly make it my custom to come to meet you as I did today. We have only to ensure that nobody sees us who might tell tales to Uncle Septimus.

'Say you will not be very cross with us when I keep you waiting. I told Elliot you would not mind helping us for he seemed worried that you might object to being so treated . . .'

'Of course, I do not,' Tamsin assured her, 'but what can you hope for by seeing him this way? It does not alter how Mrs Edgecombe and your uncle feel.'

Leonie thrust out her lower lip obstinately. 'I have tried to persuade Elliot again that we must elope, but he will not hear of it. However, I am pinning my hopes on Sir Everard. When he arrives it will be sensible that Elliot is nearby for then we can arrange an immediate meeting between the gentlemen.

'I have told Elliot he could be assured of Sir Everard's patronage once you had spoken with him, although the silly fellow fears that in Paris Sir Everard might only have been paying him polite compliments about his painting rather than offering a considered opinion. But he is too modest.

'Oh, I am convinced Sir Everard's influence will prevail over Mamma's prejudice. I have such hopes of him persuading her that Elliot has a great future as an artist. How lucky you are to be marrying a man who has the power to do so much good!'

So happy was Leonie with her own expectations she did not hear her friend sigh. Tamsin wondered how Miss Edgecombe could base her whole future on faith in Everard Fortune helping Mr James. . . .

At the rectory Tamsin was most graciously received, for Mrs Edgecombe had decided to attribute to her influence that Leonie was looking so well and cheerful and seemed to have quite recovered from that silly business with the drawing master. She received the news of her daughter's earlier encounter with Mr St John at Baden Baden with enormous interest, wondering shrewdly—but silently—how much Sir Everard might be prepared to do for this personable cousin once his own future was settled. Oh, they had been most wise to

decide to stay on at Fairford and await Sir Everard's
arrival! Like her daughter, although for different
reasons, she had great hopes of all that might be accomp-
lished through knowing Sir Everard's sweet fiancée.

It was much to Aunt Scott's credit that her niece could
sit so calmly and converse with Leonie's mamma and
uncle and aunt over a cup of China tea without any
outward sign that her heart was quite broken, or that she
considered much graver matters than the choirboys' bad
behaviour at Evensong.

If I reject his love, she mused, smiling politely as Aunt
Sophronia showed her some particularly ugly garments
she had made for the doubly-unfortunate occupants of
the foundlings' home, he might reveal everything to
Everard out of malice. Besides, she knew she could not
deny the love she felt for David St John, even if he had
none for her. Oh, she would do her duty and try to
forget, but the love would always remain. Memory of
it and Mr St John's treachery must prevent her from
learning to care for any other man—however long she
lived.

The genteel tea party was interrupted by the unexpected arrival of Mrs Scott, who looked as if she might
have run all the way from Stillwater instead of being
conveyed in the closed carriage at a brisk trot.

'I came as quickly as I could because of this calamiti-
ous news,' she gasped, her maroon bonnet somewhat
askew and her face scarlet and perspiring from haste,
shock and over-constricting stays.

She did not consider it proper to explain that when the
'calamitous news' arrived she had already loosened her
stays and was lying down in a somewhat befuddled condition so that it had taken her rather longer than normal
to assimilate all its details as well as to re-attire herself

suitably for an afternoon visit.

Aunt Sophronia offered her China tea but instead Aunt Scott accepted a glass of elderflower wine as being more beneficial in her distraught state.

'Dear lady,' the rector said in his most soothing voice, 'do calm yourself. Now, what is the trouble? You are among friends so you may tell us everything.'

'It is Sir Everard,' spluttered Mrs Scott.

Tamsin's head began to swim with a kind of sick fear.

'He has arrived,' Leonie cried excitedly.

Mrs Scott shook her head and allowed Mrs Edgecombe to straighten her bonnet, and fan her with a sheet of paper on which the rector had been jotting down some worthy sentiments for his next sermon.

'No, it is another letter.'

Tamsin looked towards her aunt in horrid expectation. Had Everard already learned of her love for his cousin and written to terminate any engagement between them as well as to forbid her his house?

'What does he say in it, ma'am?' the rector smiled reassuringly. He was well accustomed to being present whenever one of his flock had to face some trying experience and he could pride himself on possessing a suitable sentence of encouragement, advice or sympathy for every occasion.

'He has written to you too,' Tamsin's aunt told him almost triumphantly. At least, the fresh problems caused by Sir Everard could be shared. 'No doubt you will receive it tomorrow or later today.'

'To me, ma'am?' The rector did look surprised.

'Yes . . . yes. About the marriage ceremony . . .'

'He wishes me to solemnise his union with that dear young person?' The rector looked very pleased and nodded kindly towards Miss Lucas, who sat pale and still as marble awaiting the worst possible disclosure. 'How thoughtful of him. What a splendid wedding it will be.' This was better news than Leonie's uncle could have hoped for. Sir Everard and Lady Fortune would be sure to invite to Stillwater the clergyman who made them man and wife.

'No . . . no . . .' Aunt Scott positively wrung her hands with agitation, and helped herself to more elderflower wine before reflecting whether or not this was quite correct behaviour.

'What does Sir Everard write, dear aunt?' Tamsin's quiet familiar voice seemed to have the power to bring Mrs Scott to her normal self.

'Well might you ask, miss,' she snapped. 'I have never heard anything so preposterous in my life, and there is nothing that can be done to prevent this scandalous plan from taking place . . .'

'But what scandal can there be in a wedding?' the rector's wife asked sagely. In her experience the two very rarely accompanied each other, although, unfortunately, it might be whispered that sometimes a scandal occurred when a wedding was lacking. Like her husband, she was looking forward to being entertained at Stillwater and could not see any fault in the gentleman who would be their host.

'He has obtained a special licence,' Aunt Scott declared tragically, 'from the Archbishop.'

'A special licence,' echoed Mrs Edgecombe and her daughter, the former in tones of alarm, and the latter in delight.

'Then the banns do not need to be called,' explained the rector, 'but it is all perfectly legal. Under the Ecclesiastical Licences Act of 1533 . . .'

Leonie was not interested in some prosy dissertation

from Uncle Septimus on the history of the special licence. She considered Mrs Scott's 'calamitous news'
some of the most thrilling she had ever heard. Did
Tamsin not realise how lucky she was? Ah, if only she
and Elliot might be married by special licence.

'It means he does not wish to wait any longer to make
you his wife, Tamsin,' she exclaimed. 'Oh, it is so
romantic.'

'Unnecessarily so, in my opinion,' remarked her
Uncle Septimus conservatively. 'People are inclined to
make gossip out of such hurried wedding ceremonies.
There is no need for such haste. After all, nobody is
dying. Why could he not allow the arrangements to go
forward in the usual way?'

'Because he is Sir Everard Fortune,' rejoined Mrs
Scott bitterly, 'and has lived scandalously as a bachelor
and now intends to join himself in marriage to
Thomasina in a way most calculated to set tongues wag-
ging. After all I have done to preserve this child's unsul-
lied reputation . . .'

Tamsin was not thinking about her reputation. She
doubted Everard's decision to wed her as quickly as
possible had anything to do with romance—or the wish
to cause tongues to wag. No, it was more likely that he
had found himself in some sudden deep financial embarrassment which could only be removed by laying his
hands on his father's wealth with all possible speed . . .
and that required marrying her.

'When does he plan to wed dear Thomasina?' asked
Mrs Edgecombe anxiously.

'He writes that he will arrive at Stillwater tomorrow
afternoon at the latest, and will marry my niece the
following morning at eleven o'clock with the rector's
permission . . .'

'The day after tomorrow,' breathed Tamsin with loathing.

'But that leaves her no time to get a wedding dress!' observed Leonie practically. Now that was something she could not sanction. Romantic haste was all very well but a girl must look her best on her wedding day, and that would be rather difficult to achieve at such short notice. 'What on earth will you wear, dearest?' she cried.

Tamsin stared at her friend with unseeing eyes. The least of her problems was the wedding outfit. What did it matter anyway what she wore when she was to shackle herself to someone she could not love? If Everard had hoped to prevent their marriage by some cunning scheme involving his cousin his financial needs had dashed those hopes. He was unlikely to care what she wore, or whether she loved his cousin—or a whole regiment of hussars for that matter—just so long as he could possess his papa's property.

And what of David St John?

Would he be pleased that the object of his feigned affections was no longer free to be pursued? Or, perhaps he intended to continue his dalliance with a married lady. . . .

If Sir Everard cared as little for her as his wife as he had done prior to marriage he would probably prove a most complaisant husband, and look to his cousin to entertain Lady Fortune so that he would be free to lead his usual kind of life.

Tamsin had heard with repugnance that in some fashionable circles husbands made little secret of keeping mistresses and turned a blind eye to a wife's occasional infidelity so long as nobody actually gossiped about her. Since Everard was accustomed to a dissolute existence that kind of marriage would presumably not bother him, but she had no intention of allowing him to drag her so low that she could no longer respect herself.

'I expect I shall wear one of your gowns, Leonie,' she smiled wearily, 'I always do . . .' And, her mind returned to all the complications a simple ball gown had caused.

'But you must wear white,' Mrs Edgecombe wailed in great agitation. She was near tears, for weddings always made her cry, but this one seemed particularly grief-provoking.

'And where is the veil and the orange blossom?' demanded Mrs Scott gloomily. 'It is really too bad of him. I had hoped to see her properly attired for her marriage. To start married life in such a rushed and ill-prepared manner bodes little good for the future.'

'Come, dear ladies,' the rector intervened, 'I am sure so long as Miss Lucas is adequately gowned there is no call for such despondency. That the couple have affection and respect for each other is the most important factor . . .'

There was an embarrassed pause which nobody cared to fill until Leonie said cheerfully: 'But I have a white gown, have I not, Mamma? You know the one. I never wear it. Come upstairs and try it on, Tamsin. I am sure I have sufficient lace for a veil, and the Stillwater conservatories will provide you with all the flowers you need for your headdress and bouquet.'

Unhappily, Tamsin trailed after Leonie, half listening to her aunt, Mrs Edgecombe and the rector's wife begin a lively discussion of what orders should be given to the Stillwater cook with regard to a suitable wedding breakfast.

Personally, she did not care if bread and water were

served. Funeral baked meats might almost be more fitting, for there was more to mourn than to celebrate at this particular marriage.

Any discussion of Sir Everard's extraordinary behaviour was fortunately spared her because Leonie's mind was directed only to matters of fashion. She flitted about her bedroom collecting accessories which best suited the gauze afternoon gown, and soon the bed was strewn with an assortment of silk stockings, kid pumps, gloves and frothy mounds of lace and muslin petticoats, all as white as May blossom.

'It does not suit me one bit,' she assured Tamsin, hooking her into the gown. 'You had best get your maid at Stillwater to take it in at the waist for I declare you are even thinner than in London. How can that be? My appetite is shockingly improved by country air despite me being so low in spirits. Do not feel you are depriving me of a gown I like. It is far too plain. I saw it on a fashion plate and thought how pretty, but when Mamma's dressmaker had completed it I was most disappointed. Perhaps I should have chosen a more luxurious material. There . . .' she gave Tamsin a little push towards the mirror.' Strangely enough, dearest, it becomes you, but then we are so very different in temperament, are we not? You, so good and obedient, whereas I . . .' and she gave a little skip as if to demonstrate her own waywardness.

Tamsin looked in the cheval glass and saw reflected there a small, forlorn figure clad in filmy white. The gown's only trimmings were narrow lace ruffles at the throat, cuffs and hem.

'I had thought to put a three-quarter coat of blue moire over it to brighten it up,' confessed Leonie, 'but now I shall not need to go to that trouble, for you must keep the gown as all girls do after they are married. Ah, here is a scarf of Brussels lace which will serve as an adequate veil.' She draped it over Tamsin's smooth hair and admired the effect. 'Let us see what your aunt thinks of you.'

The ladies pronounced the dress and veil as perfectly acceptable, although Aunt Scott sniffed that 'The outfit was as suited to mourning as to a wedding . . .'

But the rector declared it to be modest and becoming to such a solemn ceremony. 'I do not approve of fashionable fal-lals which detract the congregation's thoughts from the true meaning of the marriage service.'

Only he was quite astonished such a dress had come from his niece's wardrobe, but less surprised that she did not choose to wear it herself.

Apparently, Mrs Edgecombe had casually remarked to Mrs Scott how the young ladies had encountered Mr St John, for she wanted to check again his exact prospects.

'I suppose the "unexpected business" which brings him hereabouts unannounced has to do with his cousin's hasty marriage plans,' snapped Mrs Scott.

'He mentioned nothing about Everard,' Tamsin assured her truthfully. 'I imagine this news will be as much a surprise to him as it is for us.'

But she could not refrain from wondering if all David St John's reasons for being so close to Stillwater were mere moonshine to hide the fact that he had only come there to expedite Everard's wedding. In which case he was most damnably toying with her love . . .

They chose to stay on at the rectory for only as long as it took Tamsin to resume her former gown.

'I doubt I shall be allowed to call on you tomorrow,' Leonie whispered regretfully, as she gathered together the items of apparel to be taken to Stillwater. 'Mamma will say you are far too busy with wedding preparations and waiting to greet Sir Everard to give me your company. Oh well, I shall see you at the church the following morning, dearest, when I may wish you happiness. I think I shall wear my new orchid silk outfit. It has the most divine silk ribbon embroidery on the jacket and hem, and I have such a cunning little hat to match.'

She did manage to squeeze a few tears from her eyes, but Tamsin thought this emotion was caused less by thoughts of the wedding and more by the knowledge that she might have lost a chance to see Mr James on the morrow.

The tears were rapidly replaced by a sunny smile. 'The sooner you are Lady Fortune,' Leonie said cheerfully, 'the sooner can my own happiness be realised. Perhaps this business of a Special Licence will bring us nothing but good.' Her soft fingers pinched Tamsin's pale cheek, 'Remember, a bridegroom will grant his new bride anything, so you might ask Sir Everard about helping Elliot as soon as you have the opportunity . . .'

She kissed Tamsin affectionately, and walked arm-in-arm with her to where Mrs Scott stood with the rector beside the carriage. It had been decided that it would be far too taxing for the bride to drive back alone, and so instead the footman would take the phaeton to Stillwater. Miss Lucas could not object, for she no longer looked for any happiness in a chance meeting with David St John.

As the carriage rattled along, Mrs Scott's own thoughts were much occupied with what outfit she should wear for the wedding and so she did not question her niece's doleful expression, but assumed it to be caused by an attack of pre-wedding nerves such as all young ladies of a modest disposition were prone to.

'At least,' she remarked in an attempt to raise the child's spirits, 'once he has arrived and you two are wed we need not always be waiting around wondering what would best please Sir Everard.'

'That,' retorted her niece with a sarcastic wit Mrs Scott had not known she possessed, 'is like welcoming your own execution because it eradicates the awful waiting . . .'

'My dear Thomasina,' Mrs Scott felt compelled to reprimand her, 'a gentleman does not appreciate a sharp-tongued wife.'

How poor Uncle Scott had shifted then, Tamsin could not imagine, for she doubted her aunt's keenness of tongue had only manifested itself with age. . . .

At Stillwater the household was in a perfect dither of delight. Even Merten's usually solemn face was split by a huge grin as he came forward to greet the ladies.

How like the master to set everybody tumbling head-over-heels to do his bidding, said the servants! A special licence just like that—what a devilish fellow Sir Everard was once he had set his mind on something! Both butler and housekeeper agreed he was a regular chip off the old Fortune block!

Even though they had but short notice for the preparations, everybody, from the humblest boothboy upwards, was determined that Sir Everard and his bride should have a wedding day they would always remember, and cook was in a state bordering frenzied jubilation as she planned how to decorate the wedding cake.

Tamsin lost no time in summoning Mary to her bedroom to attend to the necessary alterations, but before trying on the gown she had to endure the girl's flow of good wishes.

'I have never seen the master, Miss Lucas,' she prattled happily, 'nor have most of us younger servants, but we have heard what a fine gentleman he is and I am sure you and he are going to be ever so happy.'

What can I say, thought Tamsin bleakly, that will not blight this girl's trust in her master?

'Oh, by the way, miss,' Mary put a hand in her apron pocket to withdraw an envelope. 'This arrived for you not long ago.' And reverently taking the white gown over her arm, the maid hurried away to begin sewing.

This time Tamsin knew the eccentric handwriting, and almost burned the note unopened. Whatever he wrote could make no difference now.

'Tamsin, beloved, I must see you. If you value your happiness as I do, come to me at the mill as soon as you can. I shall wait there till gone midnight and if need be return again at first light.'

Underneath he had scrawled his initials.

She would not go.

There was nothing he could say that would bring her happiness.

The marriage with Everard Fortune had been arranged and must take place. Love for David St John could only bring her shame. . . .

CHAPTER
EIGHT

MRS Scott retired early, her hair tortured by a mass of curl papers, for she intended to look her best for Sir Everard's arrival. She had recommended her niece go to sleep as quickly as possible, for only rest might erase those great shadows beneath the girl's eyes.

Tamsin sat at her window watching a waxing moon rise to sail in silver splendour across the darkened countryside. Out there at the derelict mill David St John awaited her . . . to tell her what?

It was of no use. She would never sleep this night until she had heard what he wanted to say—and also taken the opportunity to tell him that she knew him for what he really was, and her love for him was entirely misconceived. . . .

Without relighting the candle Tamsin slipped out of her nightgown and donned a simple oat-meal coloured woollen day gown, for she thought the night might have a chill edge to it, and her appearance counted little for this particular meeting. Throwing a shawl over her unbound hair she crept down the great staircase.

So long as she did not encounter her aunt, roused by some stirrings of nocturnal hunger, she knew she had little to fear. The servants might wonder at her being about so late but they were busy with the wedding preparations and would be likely to assume Miss Lucas was too excited at the prospect of seeing her bridegroom to sleep and thought a moonlit stroll in the gardens might calm her. The whim of their master's future wife could be accepted with an indulgent smile. . . .

Tamsin tiptoed out of the glass doors which led on to the paved terrace, and ran lightly over the dew-soaked lawns.

The moon provided ample light to find her way to the footbridge. Only in the rustling copse was it at all dark or mysterious, but she had never felt Stillwater or its surrounding lands to be in any way frightening and so was able to continue without much feeling of apprehension.

The moon broke the surface of the millstream into a hundred silver wafers. Somewhere an owl screamed triumph in the night. So intent had Tamsin been upon what she would say to David St John that not until now had it struck her how highly improper it was to meet him in this isolated spot in total darkness. It was too late for her to reconsider and turn back, for his tall dark figure had detached itself from the shadows cast by the mill.

Warm arms embraced her tightly, and his kiss against her cheek was tender and lingering.

'Bless you for coming to me like this, my darling,' he murmured, resting his chin upon her head. Then, sensing her hostility, he held her from him at arm's length and tried to read her face.

'What is the matter, Tamsin?'

'Everything,' she spat the single word at him like a tormented, frightened animal, but continued more evenly: 'Tomorrow your cousin returns with a special licence for our wedding the following morning . . .'

'And you do not choose to marry him?'

'It is a little late for me to pretend to you that I harbour either affection or respect for Everard Fortune.'

'Then, do not marry him,' was the cool response.

Tamsin began to laugh, and her mirth was rimmed with the hysteria which accompanies desperation. 'Oh yes,' she said mockingly, 'I reside in his house, cherished by his servants, only to tell him on his arrival that I cannot marry him. How do you imagine he, or my aunt, or the rector, or the world will react to such an apparently callous rejection? I have left it a little late to withdraw from our engagement, and have nowhere to go to hide my humiliation.'

'Hear me, beloved,' David St John pleaded, 'I told you I want only your happiness, and I believe I can secure it. Marry me. If, as you say, you care nothing for wealth and title, and truly love me, you cannot say anything but "yes".'

She stared at him without understanding.

'You have told me that you love me,' he persisted, 'and you know my feelings for you.'

'Oh yes,' she admitted slowly, 'I do love you, to my cost and shame. As for you loving me, Mr St John, you care for me as much as you have done for all the other ladies you have trifled with. That is not a very sound basis for a marriage which will anyway shock our relatives and friends. What of your treatment of Leonie Edgecombe? I do not believe you would have behaved with me in the conservatory as you did . . .' and she thought how long ago that episode now seemed, '. . . if you had not already held her in your arms. Do you deny it?'

'No,' he said steadily, 'I shall never lie to you, Tamsin. It is true I have embraced your friend, but not against her will. She is something of a tease and knew very well where her flirtation must lead . . . but that is neither here nor there. That is her secret and mine, and one I hope you will keep if you care for your friend's good name. But that was before I met you. You have no cause to be jealous. If I had known you then I should not have looked at another lady, let alone made love to anyone but you . . .'

Despite herself, Tamsin's heart began to pound wildly, but her mind fought against believing him.

'And all the other ladies you have embraced and declared you adored?' she taunted.

'I am twenty-eight years old, Tamsin, and a man of flesh and blood—neither saint nor devil. I confess freely that—but how can I say this to you without causing you deep embarrassment—I have been on intimate terms with various ladies, but I have never told any of these that I loved her. You are too young and unworldly to know anything of love except as some ephemeral dream, but if you become my wife I shall teach you something of the passion that can exist between man and woman. You will have no cause ever to be jealous because I knew other ladies before I met you. . . .'

How thankful Tamsin was for the shadows, for she understood but dimly that David St John spoke of matters which were never mentioned by ladies except in behind-the-hand whispers and then not before unmarried girls.

'I did not intend to mortify you, my angel, but I had to defend myself against your accusation that I care for you only the way I have cared for others. By Heaven, that is not true.' His voice trembled as if with anger, and his grasp on her shoulders tightened. 'Lady, I would lay down my life for you if that would save you a moment's pain.'

'I have to believe you,' she whispered at last. 'But if you are misleading me I shall be the unhappiest woman ever born, for the love I bear you is so great I feel almost unable to contain it.'

'And yet you will marry a man other than me?'

She considered the alternatives. Marriage to Everard was quite impossible. The thought of submitting to his embraces now she had known David's kiss was unbearable. But if she accepted this man who had taught her the meaning of love, not only would they cause distress to all who knew them, but their life might be very uncomfortable.

'You know I have not a penny of my own,' she reminded him.

'Are you balancing the scales between riches and love?' his voice was disappointed.

She shook her head. 'No, but I am wondering if you might eventually have cause to regret marrying me. Certainly, your cousin will not help us.'

'And you, I suppose, are thinking of the jewels and gowns you will never wear, the tours you will not make, the balls you will not attend, and the fine people who will not visit you because you have no grand establishments in town and country. For you would be marrying a poor fellow whose interest is photography.

'It is true, Tamsin, I am asking you to sacrifice a great deal for me. And, what do I offer in its place: my deep, undying love, and perhaps the sort of companionship which is rare between husband and wife, for I know we can be friends as well as lovers.' His voice grew wistful, 'How I should love to see you with our first-born in your arms. What a photograph I should make of that. Tell me, sweetheart, is the world not well lost for love?'

Her only answer was to throw herself into his embrace.

'Say you will marry me,' he insisted.

'Yes, I shall marry you, Mr St John,' she whispered, and turned her face upwards for his kiss.

But instead he said briskly: 'Time enough for kisses later. We must hurry now.'

'But it is the middle of the night,' she protested.

'I cannot think of a more suitable time for eloping, can you?' David St John asked drily.

'But I have only the clothes I am wearing, and they are scarcely elegant,' she put a hand to her head where the shawl had slipped, 'even my hair is down . . .'

'What of it?'

Tamsin began to giggle weakly. She thought of Leonie who so longed to elope but whose sense of occasion demanded that she be properly attired for it. She could not imagine Miss Edgecombe fleeing in the night wearing an old gown and without at least a trunk full of suitable outfits.

'Why do you laugh?'

She told him, and it was his turn to chuckle.

'Despite her romantic streak,' he remarked shrewdly, 'she is a realistic young lady, but a dreadful minx who will lead her poor husband a merry dance.'

'And now I shall not be able to recommend Mr James to Sir Everard,' Tamsin said regretfully. She could not but agree with David's opinion that Leonie would treat Mr James rather badly once they were married unless he exhibited greater spirit.

'Tell me about that as we go,' he said, drawing her hand under his arm and hurrying her along the footpath.

Tamsin explained Leonie's expectations.

This seemed to give Mr St John great cause for mirth.

'I do not understand why you laugh, dearest,' she said severely, 'he is a most respectable young man as you would know if only you had allowed me to introduce him to you. Should Everard's opinion of his work count for anything with the rector and Mrs Edgecombe, Leonie will be allowed to engage herself to him I am sure. But, now I would imagine that Everard will look unfavourably on anyone claiming to be my friend. Oh dear, what harm I am causing by loving you . . .'

'One day I shall explain my laughter, but at present there are matters more important to consider than Miss Edgecombe and her beau. If we turn on to this other path we shall soon reach a road beyond Stillwater where my chaise is waiting.'

'But where are we going?'

'Somewhere quite safe, where I may make arrangements for our marriage, and you can refresh yourself.'

'My aunt is going to be frantic with worry when she learns I have vanished,' she said anxiously, 'and Everard will send out search parties, for it will be believed I have had some sort of accident.'

'Do not worry your head about it. I shall write to your aunt, the rector, and all those who need to be informed that Miss Lucas's plans are somewhat changed.'

'But Everard may come after us if he discovers where we are.'

'Trust me, sweetheart, that all will be well.'

The horse's ears twitched at the sound of his master's tone and it stopped cropping the turf beside the road. As he handed her into the open carriage Tamsin remarked hesitantly: 'Once Everard is recovered from the first shock and chagrin he will no doubt be relieved, for the lawyers are bound to allow him his inheritance without blaming Miss Lucas's shameful behaviour on any action of his. Do you realise you have done your cousin a great service, David St John? He may yet show you his gratitude.'

'What the devil can you mean by that, Tamsin?' he demanded, picking up the reins.

She leaned against the leather cushioning, and was suddenly aware of her complete exhaustion. 'Well,' she began slowly, 'I confess that I have often wondered if *all* the attentions you paid me were on Everard's instructions. Even now you could be eloping with me to free him and disgrace me. It could be that you have no intention of marrying me.'

The bearded profile grew hard and angry.

'Thomasina Lucas, I doubt that couples eloping usually engage in a blazing dispute, but it seems that you and I may well do so before this night turns to morning. If you really entertain such doubts of me, I shall drive you straight back to Stillwater. That I would even contemplate doing what you suspect would damn me as the most perfidious wretch ever. A Judas of the first water. Make up your mind, miss, trust me or I return you to Stillwater while there is still time.'

His very vehemence compelled her to believe him, and Tamsin said gently: 'Take me where you will, David, for my heart is already in your possession so I must needs go with it.'

How long they drove in that gentle lovers' moonlight she did not know, for the rhythm of wheels and hooves lulled her into a sound sleep she had not enjoyed for many nights.

Only when the carriage halted did she wake.

It was still dark. Faint mist veiled the ground. The night was richly perfumed with roses, honeysuckle and damp grass. The air felt sharper. A lamp burned at a window, but otherwise the building was in quiet darkness.

'Whose house is this?' she asked sleepily.

David St John lifted her down with the same ease he had used that afternoon in Oxford Street. 'It belonged to my parents,' he replied softly. 'They spent the first days of their married life here so I feel it is only fitting to bring you beneath its roof.'

It was a small house. Old, with the beams, low ceilings and great fireplaces of another age. Yet, Tamsin was aware that the furnishings and ornaments, while being old-fashioned, were certainly not rustic.

'Are there servants?' she could not but ask as the place was polished and tidy and a cold collation was neatly arranged on a white tablecloth.

'Oh, there is someone who takes care of the place,' he said, kneeling by the grate to blow on hot ashes and bring to life a small fire which warmed the room and threw leaping shadows across the walls.

Tamsin sank gratefully into a low chair, too tired to do anything but yield to surroundings so tranquil that the ticking of a clock seemed loud in contrast. I am safe here, she thought, Everard will never find me and bring me back to Stillwater.

David St John gave her a glass of claret, but she was too tired to pay any attention to the food, although she did notice that it included a delicately shaped jelly.

'Now, my little love, you must go to bed, while I write letters.'

She glanced at the small escritoire which must have belonged to a lady and could not really associate its daintiness with David St John's dreadful handwriting. Tenderly, he helped her rise and almost supported her up the steep narrow stair.

They stopped outside a door at the top of the stair-case. He opened it to reveal a most feminine bed-chamber with a silk-hung half-tester bed, a fire burning in an iron basket in the grate, and all the small comforts a lady might require.

Tamsin looked up at him a little apprehensively, aware she was alone in an empty house with a gentleman who, for all he loved her, was still a man . . . and Aunt Scott had always warned against such a contingency without specifying what might be its dire consequence.

David St John's grin was slightly rakish, as if he could read the young lady's undefined fears. He patted her cheek. 'Here is the key so you may lock your door if you believe me unprincipled enough to intrude upon your sleep. However, once the wedding ceremony is solemnised, I trust you will allow me to step over the threshold with you and close the door behind us . . .'

Modestly, she lowered her lashes but could not prevent herself from blushing or smiling. Without passion, he kissed her lips.

'Sleep well, my dear one. Try not to be too anxious about what tomorrow will bring.'

Tamsin thought she would never sleep, for she could not but think of what Sir Everard would do if he caught up with them . . . and what terrible aspersions her aunt and the world would cast upon her headlong flight. . . .

But she did sleep, and awoke to birdsong and bright sunshine, momentarily wondering where she was. The events of the previous night surged back, and she wondered how she had found the courage to accept David St John's proposal.

Tamsin lay there, knowing herself to be quite helpless and in his power whatever he chose to do. It seemed to her that Leonie's irresponsible view of elopement as a thrilling and romantic adventure was quite inappropriate. Rather, it was a grave step from which there was no turning back.

There came a gentle knocking at the door. Knowing

she had finally decided not to lock it, Tamsin called: 'Enter.'

A very old lady, bearing a breakfast tray, gave the girl a curious little smile, so that Tamsin almost felt like a naughty child who deserved a scolding but instead would be given a sweetmeat and a hug. She had not known this feeling since her dear papa died.

'The master says you're to make a good breakfast, miss. I shall bring you hot water for washing as soon as you have eaten all this, and will help you with your hair . . .' she added severely: 'It needs a thorough brushing, young lady.'

With a hunger she had not previously recognised, Tamsin devoured the hot, white rolls, the butter and gooseberry preserve and drank all the coffee contained in the elegant silver pot. In a silver porringer under a mound of thick yellow cream she discovered strawberries.

She was eating these when another brief knock at the door revealed David St John. He stood in the doorway, and Tamsin noticed that he looked somewhat tired.

'I trust you slept well, my love. I am pleased to see you have obeyed my wishes with regard to breakfast. If you are always so obedient we should shift marvellously together.'

'But I was pleasing myself at the same time as doing your bidding.'

'Then I must ascertain that I only require of you what you would choose yourself,' he said seriously. 'The letters are written and dispatched which is why I have had but little sleep. I should be obliged if you would be ready by eleven o'clock. My old nurse will help you.'

'Is she the person who looks after this house?'

He nodded. 'And if you draw her out on the subject

she will tell you that I was a most headstrong child and have not changed a whit . . . but she will only reveal that once we are married, for she would not wish to deter you, since she believes strongly I am in need of a wife.'

'In that she and I are agreed.'

'And she has already expressed her opinion on my choice of bride,' he pressed a finger against his smiling lips.

'What is that?'

'Oh, Miss Lucas is well enough but her hair is untidy.'

'Once again I shall not dispute with her,' and ruefully Tamsin added: 'Alas, even with my hair neatly arranged I shall be most dowdily dressed.'

'As to that, I have a gown which I believe may fit you pretty well, although you will find its style extremely old-fashioned. Please wear it.'

So intrigued was she by his mention of a gown that Tamsin forgot to ask him why eleven o'clock had any significance. As soon as the nurse brought in the hot water she hastened to begin her toilette.

While she washed the old woman rummaged in a chest of drawers to produce laundered delicate undergarments, clocked silk stockings, and even a pair of small kid slippers which were approximately the size of Miss Lucas's feet.

Tamsin might have been rather suspicious as to why David St John possessed such a selection of female garments had they all not belonged to another age, as had the long-sleeved, collared nightgown she had found spread out upon the bed the previous night. Everything, her nose delightedly noted, had been laid in lavender.

With a dexterity which belied her gnarled appearance, the nurse's hands set about brushing Tamsin's hair until it gleamed and then dressed it to both their satisfaction.

At last, from the press she took a gown—a confection of gauze over a silken bodice and petticoat with the most elaborate scalloped Gabrielle sleeves and a deep round neck. Once it had been white but age had turned the silk to ivory.

'It is the most beautiful dress I have ever seen,' breathed Tamsin, stroking the soft, shimmering cloth with reverent hands. She doubted even Miss Edgecombe would fault its rich quality.

The old woman said nothing but fastened her into the gown. David St John had not been wrong. The original owner may have been taller than Tamsin, since the gown was intended to be ankle-length rather than sweep the floor, but otherwise they shared a similar slenderness.

Still unspeaking, the nurse gave Tamsin's cheek a dry peck and brushed tears from her own eyes. 'He is waiting for you downstairs, little miss. Go to him.'

Feeling somewhat strange in her rustling finery, Tamsin descended to the parlour where a gentleman stood gazing through the casement. At the sound of her footfalls he turned.

For an instant she could have believed that David St John had vanished to be replaced by a strange gentleman, sober and elegant in dark grey. Yet the smiling eyes were as ever . . . only the features, devoid of beard and moustaches, were more handsome and commanding than she could have imagined.

Tamsin's fingers fluttered to her mouth to conceal the little gasp of surprise.

'I had a fancy to return to my clean-shaven state,' said Mr St John lightly, 'I trust you do not find my transformation too displeasing.'

'Oh no . . . not at all.' She hoped he could not guess that her blush was caused by a brief speculation as to what it would feel like to receive kisses from lips no longer surrounded by bristles. 'It is most becoming.'

'My appearance is unimportant,' he countered smiling. 'Yours is everything. I fear you will find this bonnet a trifle old-fashioned although it was made to match the gown.' Very gently he placed a little confection of gauze and lace upon her curls and most deftly tied the ribbons beneath her chin.

'You are as cunning with your hands as any lady's maid,' Tamsin laughed. 'I had no intimation that gentlemen understood such matters.'

'We learn on our cravats,' he assured her grinning, but then his face grew serious. 'You are truly beautiful,' he said, taking her by the hand.

'I am not. It is this wonderful gown and bonnet. To whom did they belong?'

'My mother,' David St John returned quietly, and Tamsin understood the riddle of the lady's clothes in her bedroom.

'You have everything so well arranged for my comfort,' she observed half laughing, 'did you know for sure I would run away with you?'

He shook his head. 'No, but I had hoped you would.'

'Where are we going so finely dressed?'

'You will understand when we arrive. Now I want to show you something.'

He produced the photograph taken by the mill.

Tamsin clapped her hands in delight and confessed ingenuously: 'I did not know I could look so pretty. My looking-glass does not pay me the compliments of your clever camera.'

He smiled at her pleasure. 'Now David St John has a lasting record of the day Tamsin Lucas said she loved him, no matter what befalls.'

'That is most romantic of you,' she teased. 'But you will have the living proof of it by your side.'

'Ah, very soon you may change your mind about loving me,' he rejoined, and she looked up at him expecting to see a smile, but his face was very grave, as if he indeed meant what he said.

'How foolish you are!' she scolded. 'I am unlikely to reconsider my love for you.'

He shook his head. 'I hope I may believe you.'

'But what is wrong that makes you think me fickle-hearted?' Tamsin cried. 'I would scarcely agree to run away with you, only to say on the following day I have changed my mind and quite mistaken my affection.'

'We shall see.' David St John's drawl sounded curiously unconvinced. 'Now let me show you another picture of yourself—not as sharp or as well composed but still a lasting momento . . .'

Tamsin gazed in bewilderment at the blurred image which was undoubtedly herself, for she recognised the small bonnet and short cape that she had worn in London.

'But how is this possible? I do not remember you with any camera.'

'I have told you how I am working on the construction of a concealed camera. This is one of its first efforts. You did not know you were being photographed that day in Connaught Square.'

'Where was the camera hidden?'

'In one of my walking sticks.'

'Did you do it for Everard?' she asked suspiciously, wondering if he had perhaps thought to give his cousin a record of her stepping out of the house without a chaperone.

His grin was faintly sardonic. 'Why not? How could I

be sure a day would come when Miss Lucas actually consented to be photographed.'

He took the watch from its pocket in his light grey silk waistcoat and consulted it. 'We must go or we shall be late.'

'I do not know where we are,' Tamsin remarked vaguely as they drove away from the house which daylight showed to be set in pretty, well-tended gardens, and she could not help thinking that at least they would have a home when they eventually married. 'All these narrow roads look alike to me. Are we far from Gloucestershire?'

But he seemed not to hear her question.

From time to time, Tamsin stole perplexed little glances at her silent companion, and wondered why he was so withdrawn, almost unhappy, as if he had begun to doubt the wisdom of their love.

At last, he said: 'We are nearly there.'

Ahead stood a handsome grey stone church with a Romanesque tower proclaiming its antiquity. The chaise halted in a lane beside the churchyard which ran down to a lazy curve of river. A tranquil English country scene enhanced by a perfect summer's day.

'Are we going into that church?'

He nodded.

'But why?'

'Can you not guess?'

Her eyes sheened with tears of happiness. 'Do you mean we are to be married this very day?'

'If you will agree to it, Tamsin.'

She clasped her hands, wondering why it was possible to laugh and weep at one time. 'How can you doubt that? Now, I understand why we are dressed so finely. Oh, I am so happy. I thought we might have to wait and in that

waiting Everard and my aunt would try to force us apart.
How have you managed to arrange matters with such
speed?'

Very gently, he helped her descend from the carriage.
'You will see,' was all he would say, and took her by the
hand to lead her along the worn, flagged path into the
porch.

David St John pushed open the heavy wooden door to
allow her to enter ahead of him.

The noon sun struck jewel-bright through the lofty
decorated windows so that the stone floor was stained
with patterns of deepest blue, crimson and gold. For an
instant Tamsin was too dazzled to see properly. She
noticed the church was decorated with masses of lilies
and small pink roses, as if in readiness for some fashionable wedding.

Near the altar rail waited a knot of people looking
towards her expectantly.

Tamsin stood so still she appeared a pale figurine
under that vaulted soaring roof.

He had betrayed her.

It had all been a monstrous deception after all to
deliver her into the clutches of his cousin.

For she knew these people: Aunt Scott, in her best
maroon casaweck with the little ermine collar over a
matching gown; Mrs Edgecombe, pink-cheeked and
pretty under a blue plumed bonnet; Leonie, quite
radiant in the orchid outfit she had mentioned; her Aunt
Sophronia in a too-vivid purple—and there was the
rector in white and black, book in hand, as if waiting to
conduct a service. Standing in a pew not far behind
Leonie she recognised Elliot James, solemn but surprisingly at ease for someone so outlawed in that company.
There were also two elderly gentlemen in dark coats,

whose grave faces she did not know.

Then, all smiled to see her, and there was not even the shadow of a condemnatory glare in her aunt's gaze.

As she stood there, bewildered, Leonie came forward holding out a delicate bouquet of white lilies, orange blossom and pink roses tied with white silk streamers. She thrust it into Tamsin's hands. 'There, darling, you must have your flowers. How truly beautiful you look. What a happy day this is.'

Tamsin swayed. She would have fallen, but a man's hand caught her elbow and she looked up to see David St John's face. His skin was very pale and stretched against the darkness of his hair.

'What have you done to me?' her cry echoed through the church. 'You have handed me to your cousin. But where is he? I thought he would not arrive until this afternoon for is not the wedding arranged for tomorrow morning? Surely, you are all a little prematurely gathered together . . .'

'With a special licence one may alter dates,' he said quietly.

'You—my betrayer—and I loved you so much . . .' she said brokenly. What difference could it make now that everyone should know this fact?

Firmly, he led her towards the rail, and she thought: I am like a sacrificial lamb being brought to the slaughter. She expected some reproving glance from her aunt, and was dimly aware that the lady's face was quite tear-stained and she had broken a rule of a lifetime by wearing face powder. As if trying to encourage her niece to be brave she managed a tremulous smile.

Tamsin was tempted to pull free, and dash down the aisle and out of that church. She would run until she dropped. As if he guessed these wild thoughts, David St

John's clasp tightened on her arm.

'Ladies and gentlemen,' his voice was firm against the silence, 'I have something to say to Miss Lucas which must be witnessed by you all so there are no future misunderstandings . . .'

'There is nothing left for you to say to me,' Tamsin interrupted bitterly. 'Judas!'

'No, Miss Lucas, you must hear what I have to say,' David St John insisted. 'Then judge me . . . and on that judgment I shall stand condemned or pardoned . . .'

The dark eyes that had looked so intently into hers as they embraced now pleaded with her to listen.

'It is true, as you have always suspected, that Everard Fortune had no wish to marry you, but knew his inheritance depended upon so doing. Oh, he thought of many schemes for wriggling out of his duty, and is an astute enough fellow to have discovered some loophole whereby he could realise his property and disembarrass himself of the lady,' he smiled wanly towards the two sombre-coated gentlemen, 'despite the advice of his good friends and lawyers, Mr Graveney and Mr Hampden.

'But there was also curiosity about this girl he was supposed to wed. He had only a dim unhelpful memory of her as a child, and had heard she had been strictly reared and was probably somewhat insipid and prudish . . .' Here he had the grace to look sheepishly at Mrs Scott.

'So he thought he would attempt to find out what manner of person she was, and if she was just another young female willing to sell herself into loveless matrimony for title and money, while pretending it was duty rather than self-interest. But how was he to make these investigations into her character without her knowledge? She was unlikely to reveal her true self to Everard Fortune if she believed her future depended upon behaving in a way he could not fault . . .

'To his disbelief and delight he was shortly to discover she was quite another sort of lady—a rare kind—whom he would be proud and happy to make his wife, only by then it was too late, for she had begun to care for another . . .'

Angrily, Tamsin shook her aching head. He was talking in riddles which excused nothing.

Positively bubbling with excitement which could no longer be suppressed even by the presence of her uncle, Leonie Edgecombe almost shrieked: 'Dearest, can't you understand? Oh, it is vastly romantic. Sir Everard pretended to be your Mr St Johr., and in that guise fell in love with you . . . and you—you wicked creature for not confiding in me—fell in love with him, thinking all the while that you were neglecting your proper duty . . .'

Then, she added more thoughtfully, as if the knowledge had just dawned upon her: 'So it was Sir Everard I actually encountered in Baden Baden—if only I had known . . .' but here, Miss Edgecombe grew reticent.

'What are you saying?' Tamsin's eyes were wild storms, and her voice had the quality of distant thunder. Not since the days of childhood had she been so furious.

'That I am Everard Fortune, Tamsin, yet I dared not reveal that fact lest you begin to hate me for deceiving you and seeming to test your character by showing you all the benefits that would be yours if you became Lady Fortune. Yet those worldly prospects mattered little to you, for you preferred the attentions of an impoverished inventor . . .

'But, in London I began to fear that although I had

grown a beard to disguise my appearance some of the many folk I had met on my travels would recognise me. Remember how I hurried you away from the Exhibition. I knew those gentlemen. By their expressions I vow they had seen through my disguise. Thus, Sir Everard commanded you to go to stay at Stillwater, where I could not even visit you in case some of the older servants recognised me. Although I could rely on their loyalty to protect my secret I was still fearful the truth might be made known to you accidentally.

'Only in the countryside of my childhood did I realise how I had tricked myself. The cousin you loved and the man you hated were one and the same . . . one writing almost illegibly with his left hand so that you would not realise that he was also the gentleman who had communicated with you in a more normal handwriting. I dreaded to tell you the truth in case your loathing for Everard outweighed any love of David. You might decide that this deception was sufficient proof of Everard's viciousness.

'In order to precipitate you into an elopement Everard had to set a date for the wedding. I doubt you would have fled with me last night had it not been for his imminent arrival to claim you as his bride. When you accused me of doing everything for Everard's sake, Tamsin, you spoke more truly than ever you knew.

'Last night, while you slept, I delivered those letters I had written in Everard's hand. We were never far from Fairford or Stillwater, although of course you could not be expected to realise that, so it did not take too long for me to drive to the rectory where most kindly the rector agreed to marry us one day earlier than planned, and then, I must confess in some trepidation, I went on to Stillwater to waken your aunt, who, all blessings to her wisdom, generously forgave me once I had assured her you were quite safe. Both she and the rector, however . . .' his smile was contrite, 'pointed out just how stupidly I had behaved.

'While in Fairford I naturally took the opportunity to invite our friends, Mrs Edgecombe and her daughter, to the wedding, and of course the rector's good lady. I had already sent word of my plans to my solicitors, for I desired Mr Graveny to give away the bride and Mr Hampden to act as a witness. Since they had both been present when our papas signed their wills it seemed only right that they should see the conditions fulfilled.

'As Elliot James is known to both of us and happened to be in the neighbourhood I hoped he would do me the honour of acting as another witness, for I should like to commission him to paint my wife's portrait—that is, if I have a wife. You will understand why I avoided meeting him that afternoon in Connaught Square when I explain that I feared his artist's eye might straightaway recognise the man he had already known in Paris.'

Tamsin could not fail to notice how Leonie smiled with triumph at a blushing Mr James, and even her mamma appeared quite gratified that the drawing master was of sufficient account to attract Sir Everard's patronage.

'But there still remained a major problem. I cannot marry you by trickery, Tamsin. It is impossible for Mr St John to detach himself from Sir Everard Fortune so you must decide whether or not you will marry Everard.

'Believe me, should you decline, no shame or breath of scandal will taint your reputation. Before God and this congregation I declare you innocent of any fault. For me, your refusal can only mean the deepest grief. If I lose my inheritance so be it,' he glanced at her implacable face, and sighed wearily for he had already lost hope of happiness. 'that is no more than I deserve. Fortune's folly, the world will jestingly call it. Through my imposture I discovered the one woman I would marry and through it I lost her and everything else . . .'

There was a silence which even the rector did not break; for once he had no words suited to such an extraordinary situation. The church door creaked open and Tamsin turned to see the old nurse hobble in and sit in a pew near the back. Only then did she notice the servants from Stillwater, and others she supposed to be tenants, filled many of the pews.

'Will you marry me, Tamsin? Please,' his voice sounded as if it came from faraway.

All eyes rested anxiously on the dainty figure of Sir Everard Fortune's bride and willed her to answer in a way which would bring them all happiness.

Tamsin knew she could say no. Indeed, she opened her lips to form that single word of complete rejection.

But . . .

It was impossible.

Life would not be worth living without David St John even though his true name was Everard Fortune.

'I shall marry you on one condition, Everard Fortune,' and she thought how odd it was to address him by any name other than David. Mrs Scott looked incredulous that her biddable little niece could sound so obdurate.

'Anything in the world,' he promised.

'You dragged me from London before I had seen the Exhibition properly. I wish to spend part of our honeymoon in London rectifying that deprivation. After all, I have a season ticket which is being wasted . . .'

The faces of those around her collapsed into surprised

but delighted smiles, and there was even a ripple of laughter from the servants' pews. The master had found a young lady who would manage him perfectly . . .

'Oh, Tamsin, my darling,' Everard's shout of laughter contained a sob of relief. 'If you wish, we shall go there every day until it closes.'

He pulled her to him, not caring if he crumpled gown or bonnet. Before the shocked gaze of Mrs Scott and the rector's wife, and the more sympathetic eyes of all others, he kissed her on the lips.

For a brief second both of them forgot there were any other people in the world.

Then the rector coughed meaningfully, and his mellifluous voice interrupted: 'Sir Everard and Miss Lucas, if you are quite ready, I shall begin . . .

'*Dearly beloved, we are gathered together here in the sight of God, and in the face of this congregation, to join this man and this woman in Holy Matrimony . . .*'

And Tamsin knew the ceremony could not be performed swiftly enough so much did she now long to be Everard Fortune's wife.

What makes

**Masquerade**

books so exciting?

Engrossing plots...realistic, interesting characters...fascinating historical settings...but most of all *love*, pure, once-in-a-lifetime true love, the kind you always dreamed about.

Your heart is the target... so beware!